MW00964620

# YOU WILL DIE

**Anna-marie Morgan**

## Dedication

To my wonderful son, Christopher.

Edited: David Burton, Economyedits.wordpress.com, 2016

Cover: SelfPubBookCovers.com/Shardel

*'Come here my friends, behould and see*

*Suche as I am, suche shall ye be*

*As is my state, within this tombe*

*So must be yours before the doome*

*Even dust, as I am now*

*thou, in time, shall be.'*


*Anon  (old English)*

**ONE**

Ear-splitting thunder shredded the sky, like a bandage torn for the wounded. He cowered instinctively, as though the entire wrath of God was aimed at him, and him alone. The veins in his temples made tents in his fragile skin, as he struggled to cover the last hundred yards to the street lamp. He examined the note again, turning it over in cold-stiffened hands.

*Reverend Evans, I need to speak with you, urgently. Please come to St. David's church at 9.00 pm.*

The note revealed nothing about the sender. Outside of the locked church, David Evans found himself alone. It was 9.15 pm.

Jagged rapiers of light rendered the building in stark facade. Light and shade. Good and evil. A rogue sapling, growing from a hole in the main tower, appeared dwarfed by its own gnarled shadow, dancing grotesquely in the flickering light.

The wind flapped the note in his hand and chilled the inside of his coat, as a large raindrop hit him hard on the top of his head, followed by another and another. Within moments, the downpour was torrential and he sought shelter in the church doorway, closing his eyes.

"Hello, Father." The deep, rasping voice was barely audible above the rain, the wind and the thrashing of branches.

"Hello?" He stumbled forward, searching for the voice's owner.

4

Forked lightening illuminated long grass, discarded bottles and broken roof tiles.

"Where are you? I can't see you..." The reverend's head thrashed like the branches. He held the rain-soaked note above his head in a futile attempt at shelter.

A hooded shadow appeared on the path and crept eerily up the church wall.

He cowered again. "Who are you? What do you want?" His abdominal muscles clenched so tight, they might render him in two.

"You."

"Me?" He could taste the iron-tang of blood, as his own teeth dug into his fist.

The figure leapt forward, grabbing the reverend by the shoulders, thrusting paper into his face. "Read."

"W...What...?"

"Read." The staccato word was delivered by a voice thick with violence.

Fingers, like steel rods, shot pain through his shoulders, and he fought for breath, squinting in the dim light and heavy rain. When he swallowed, it felt like he was swallowing his fist. A blinding torch shone on him and the page he was holding. All else was deep shadow. He didn't dare look into the shadow.

"*Through the ages, Almighty God has moved His people to...*"

"Kneel."

He sank to his knees in the cold, dank mud. "*...build houses of prayer and praise...*"

"Louder."

"...and to set apart places for the ministry of His holy word and sacraments. With gratitude for the adornment of St. David's church, w...we are now gathered to dedicate and consecrate it in God's name."

"Now the prayer."

He could feel the mud splashing his face as the rain plowed down around him. The sky lit up again and the ensuing thunder all but drowned out his next few words.

"Let us pray. Almighty God, we thank you for making us in Your image, to share in the ordering of Your world.  Receive the work of our hands in this place, now to be set apart for Your worship, the building up of the living, and the remembrance of the dead, to the praise and glory of Your name; through Jesus Christ, our Lord. Amen."

As he finished reading, he had visions of his congregation: could see the respect they afforded him and the pleasure they took from the reassurance of the sermon. They were singing and praising God. The sound was beautiful to him.

Something hard smashed against his skull, the singing replaced by the sound of the blood coursing through and out.  His cracked voice howled in pain, as the thick, warm fluid snaked down his neck, mixing with the muddy rain.  It was the last worldly thing he felt. The killer dragged his body to the bushes at the back of the church, ripping the blood-stained collar from his neck with gloved hands.

*

6

Making sure he was unobserved, the killer placed a clean collar at the foot of the church door, putting the freshly bloodied one in a plastic bag, in his holdall. He spent several minutes with the body, and made the most of every one, in order to leave his message. Peeling off the gloves, he placed them in his pocket and set off through the back of the churchyard to the car park.

## TWO

"Diolch yn fawr, ma'am!" DS Dewi Hughes grinned and ducked, as he took the open file from his DI.

"Dewi Hughes, I didn't come here to learn Welsh." Yvonne raised her right eyebrow, but couldn't resist the curl of a smile at her detective sergeant's wicked eyes.

"What does it *mean,* anyway?" She poured herself a coffee.

"It means, thank you very much, ma'am." Dewi passed her the milk.

Yvonne, still adjusting to her new life, fingered the two inch scar on her chin, the result of injuries sustained at the hands of the Shotover Sadist. Her jaw had long since mended, but it ached sometimes. Dewi watched her rub her chin, his gaze soft, but he knew better than to ask if she was all right.

The decision to transfer to another force area had been hard but necessary. A fresh start. A slower pace of life. A balm to her shattered psyche. Her fifty-year-old DS,
with his endearing Welsh lilt, had welcomed her warmly and she felt oddly at home.

There was a lot to get used to: dual language paperwork; dual language road signs; complicated budgets from the The Senedd and Whitehall. Overall, though, the experience had been a positive one and Yvonne was feeling more herself than she had in a while.

8

"What's going on?" Yvonne strode into the main office, in response to the rapidly increasing noise level. "Fill me in," she ordered, putting her coffee to one side.

"There's a body, ma'am, down at St. David's church." The young DC Clayton glanced at his notes. "It's a bit of a mess by all accounts. DCI Llewelyn asked that you get down there, ASAP."

The DI stiffened. "Foul play?"

"Look's like it."

"I'm on it. Dewi?"

"Coming, ma'am."

The church was only a ten minute drive. Five minutes with lights and sirens. SOCO officers were already cordoning off the area and erecting a small marquee. They handed Yvonne a paper suit and plastic overshoes and she crouched to look at the body.

The victim was fully clothed, but his jacket and shirt had been slashed open, baring his torso. His chest and abdomen had been roughly carved with what looked like words. These were indecipherable due to a mass of congealed blood. A cross could just be made out at the end of the script. His face was contorted, the eyes and mouth wide open.

A WPC, standing behind the DI, shook her head. "Made a mess of him, didn't he, ma'am?"

"I'm sorry, I don't know your name." Yvonne stood to full height again, her gaze pensive, lips pursed.

"Watkins, ma'am. Marie Watkins."

"Yes, he did, Marie," she sighed. "Yes, he did."

9

"They found a priest's collar at the back door, ma'am, and this piece of paper clasped in the dead man's hand." Dewi passed her a plastic evidence bag. "The only other thing found was a plank of wood. SOCO have that already."

Yvonne examined the bloodied piece of paper, through the evidence bag. It had been torn from a book and was yellowed with age. The wording was religious, as was the marking on the corpse. The DI took a photo with her mobile.

**THREE**

He fastened his white breeches, snapping the braces into place on his shoulders. They hugged his shape. He smiled at his reflection in the mirror, before pulling on his plastron: 800 newtons of top notch, underarm protection. He intended to press his

opponent hard. The metal-covered jacket, and his leather glove, finished the ensemble. Time to go.

He grabbed his mask and foil and strode out into the hall, where his adversary leaned against the wall, looking bored.

They linked up to their respective boxes, pulling the metal wires and clipping them into their jackets. Extending arms, they touched their foil ends, to see the red and green bulbs flash. His light was red. He preferred red. Foil blades to noses in salute, masks on heads, and the bout was on.

They streaked back and forth on their improvised piste, fast and furious, fighting for dominance. They were well-matched. Thrust, parry, riposte. Their footwear squeaked on the polished, wooden floor, as perspiration further increased the humidity.

'Beep', the green light flashed. He whipped his weapon through the air, gritting his teeth as they returned to their start positions. Straight away, he threatened, arm extended, avoiding the parry by lunging underneath. He was deeply satisfied when he saw the red bulb flash.

The bout took longer than usual, but the final point gave him the most satisfaction: his blade bent almost double into the padded chest of the other. Each stepped back, removing their masks, hair wet and curled with the sweat of the match. Eyes locked, they saluted again and bowed.

Quick as a flash, his foil thrust towards his opponent's head, the rubber tip landing right between the eyes of his rival, who gasped at the unexpected gesture. The aggressor cocked his head to one side, examining the way the point of his foil depressed the other man's skin with concentric ripples. Then, stepping back thoroughly relaxed, he brought the foil back down to his side. "Just testing."

His opponent's shock was replaced with a smile which did not reach his eyes.

Yvonne stood on the threshold of a modest cottage, taking in the neat flower beds, tidy lawn, and the views over Newtown. Nestled in the valley of the River Severn, this was where the Reverend David Evans had chosen to spend his last years. She paused, before rapping the knocker twice.

The door was opened by a silver-haired lady in her mid-to-late fifties. Her eyes were red-rimmed and her hand held an empty mug.

"Hello...Mrs Evans? DI Yvonne Giles, Dyfed-Powys police." Yvonne's eyes

12

were genuinely earnest. They lingered on the wooden masks adorning the walls, as she was led through the hallway into the lounge.

"I'm not Mrs Evans," the other finally said. "The reverend was widowed ten years ago. I'm Sandra, the cleaner. I come here twice a week, most weeks. I'm waiting for his daughter to arrive. She's coming here from Devon."

"I see, I'm sorry, I mistook..."

"It's okay."

"And I'm sorry for your loss."

Sandra nodded.

"A team will be here shortly to go through the house. I apologise for the disruption this will cause, but we need to move quickly if we are going to find his killer."

Sandra let out a sob.

"When did you last see him?"

"Two days ago. That would have been Tuesday morning."

"How did he seem?"

"Same as always. He was his usual cheery self."

"Do you know why he was up at the church? I understand the church hasn't been in use for some years."

Sandra shook her head. "I don't know, officer. I know he missed his old life - missed the congregation."

"How did he spend his time?"

"He travelled a lot. In fact, he's...I mean he'd...only recently returned from Africa."

"Africa?"

"Yes, he said he'd visited missionary outposts there. Now I think about it, he seemed distracted, when I saw him on Tuesday."

"Any idea what might have been distracting him?"

"No. He had Alzheimer's. He'd had it a while before it was diagnosed last year. He had lucid times, and times when he thought he was still preaching. His daughter will probably tell you more."

Yvonne made a note to discover more about the African trip and the extent of his Alzheimer's. "One of my officers will be over later to talk to his daughter," she said softly. "I expect she'll be devastated."

Sandra sighed, and Yvonne sensed it was time to leave. "Please don't move his belongings, Sandra. And I think it best you don't clean for the time being."

Sandra murmured in agreement as saw the detective out.

She straightened her skirt, took a deep breath, and gave the door two firm raps.

"Come in." Forty-two-year old DCI Christopher Llewelyn was standing with his back to the door, gazing out of his office window. Hands behind his back, he turned towards her, his movement unhurried. "Yvonne." He nodded the clipped greeting.

"I just got back, sir."

14

He ran a hand through his coal-black hair, soft grey developing at the temples. The cleft in his chin appeared more prominent than usual as it was highlighted by the sun. Curious green eyes searched her face. "Was it bad?"

"Quite bad, sir. The locals are in shock."

"Robbery?"

"I don't believe so. The reverend's wallet was still in his jacket pocket."

"Motive?"

"None yet...we're still awaiting postmortem results." Yvonne cleared her throat, feeling the blood surface in her cheeks, as the DCI stared silently at her for several seconds.

"How are you settling in?" he asked.

Surprised at the change of subject, she shifted from one foot to the other. "So far, so good. I've been made very welcome and everything seems to be falling into place."

"Good. I'll make sure you have the assistance you need on this investigation. Come and talk if you need to and, obviously, I want you to keep me informed every step of the way." He smiled warmly. "It's good to have you on board."

15

The smell of cleaning and sterilisation fluids was familiar, even if this particular  mortuary room was not. The pathologist, Roger Hanson, was already at work as she

arrived. The body had been cleaned.

"DI Giles?" He peered over the top of his glasses.

"That's me, I'm sorry, I aimed to get here earlier." She hurried to his side.

"No matter, I haven't long been here myself."

Her attention turned to the dead man on the table. She drew in her breath. The reverend's face was a contorted testament to the horror he had felt at the moment of death, his eyes bloodshot, his mouth wide open. The mutilations on his chest and abdomen, now free of blood, gave a clear message from the killer.

Below the rough cross gouged in his chest were two words, their carving rough

but readable.

"Memento Mori..." Yvonne said, leaning in close.

"My Latin is rusty, these days, but this one's easy - remember death, *or* remember you will die. The wounds are not deep, and they are clearly only there for the benefit of anyone viewing the body."

"And I hoped I'd seen the last of murderous attention seekers," she sighed. "How did he die?"

"Severe blunt trauma to the head." Hanson pointed to the obvious injury. "It's no mystery as regards the weapon: a bloodstained, oak plank was found next to the body, in the churchyard. He was hit with the side of it. There's an indentation which fits exactly. One blow, which cracked the skull and, I suspect, caused massive brain hemorrhage. I'll confirm once I open it up."

"How long did the killer spend with the body, in your estimation?"

"Ooooh, probably not that long. It would have taken no more than a few minutes to create these mutilations. They're pretty rough."

"Thank you, Roger." Yvonne shuddered. Gazing down at the victim, she wondered if his disease might have protected him from the worst of it. His frozen death mask suggested not.


Later that evening, Yvonne sat with a glass of white and a headache. She rubbed her eyes, read through her notes from the day, and examined the crime scene photographs. It wasn't long until her shattered body gave in to sleep.

He barely had time to notice the powdered stone dislodged from the oldchurch wall before the second bullet entered the left side of his chin, fracturing his jaw and exiting to the back-right-hand-side of his neck.

Knees buckling beneath him, he looked in the direction of the shooter before collapsing - like a building in a controlled explosion - to the ground.

He could hear someone running towards him, and felt the kicked-up dust in his mouth. He tried calling out, but managed only a desperate gurgling.

The sun was high, searing, blinding. With each spasm the pain diminished. He could only just make out the dark shape moving in close, slashing at his clothing and chest. Finally, the all-enveloping light came. It welcomed him home to his God and to peace.

The killer breathed hard and deep, wiping his weapon on the reverend's torn clothing, before ripping the blood-stained collar from his victim's lifeless neck. He placed it in a plastic zip-lock bag. He paused, observing the blood becoming invisible on the black cloth, then set about arranging the body.

Taking two plastic bags from his pocket, he extracted from one a previously bloodied collar which he placed at the foot of the church door. He took more props from yet another bag and left them in various places on the dead man.

A quick check around, and he left the walled churchyard, striding to his waiting truck. He placed the rifle in his leather holdall along with the blade.

## FOUR

Yvonne chewed her fingers, while Dewi sighed every few minutes.

"Damn, I really thought I might get a chance then." Dewi leaned to his right, peering ahead, waiting for a gap.

"Try flashing your lights at him." Yvonne couldn't see anything save the back of the horse box. In an unmarked police car, they had no advantage over any other Joe. It felt like a lifetime until they took an opportunity to overtake. Dewi pressed his foot so hard on the accelerator, they shot past the horsebox, quickly leaving the farmer behind.

"Thank goodness for that." Yvonne breathed again.

On any other day, she would have enjoyed the journey to Llwyngwril. The hills and crags - some wooded, some bare - stood as the magnificent backdrop for the dry stone walls, lively streams, and the creatures in the fields. But news of another murder had ripped at the gut of the DI and her sergeant, and they just needed to be there.

They were greeted by a scene of stark contrasts. The old church stood in its own grounds, at the edge of the land. A stunning view lay ahead, over the bay and ocean. In front of this, at the foot of the iron-gated entrance, lay the crumpled body. SOCO personnel had just arrived and plastic suits were everywhere, processing the scene.

"Who was he?" Yvonne's hand trembled as she lifted the blue and white cordon to step under it, her eyes not leaving the body.

"Reverend George Jones."  A local constable guided Yvonne through the SOCO markers.  "He'd just delivered a sermon at another church.    Err..."    He checked his notes.    "The newer church in Llangelynin.  He'd come down here to prepare for his monthly sermon at the old church.  It was due to take place this evening."

The bulging eyes of the shattered corpse appeared as though begging for help, even now.  The  warm day felt suddenly cold.  Dewi approached them from the road.

"His clerical collar, Dewi, where is it?"  She knelt close to the body.  "Apparently, he had just finished a sermon.  Check the church door."

Her hunch proved correct, a bloodied collar was found and taken by SOCO.  One of their number addressed her.  "The victim had pies in his pockets...pasties, I think, and several of them."

"Meaning what?"  Yvonne stood up, raising her eyebrows.  "Did he have a *thing* for pasties?"

"Don't know until you guys have talked to the relatives.  Local uniform are out talking to parishioners."

"Hmmmm."    Yvonne turned her attention to the old church, its outline rugged against the backdrop of the sea, tranquil and ancient. Well-worn. She passed through the arched gateway, onto the narrow pathway leading to the church door.

"The church warden is inside, ma'am."  A WPC stepped back to allow the DI to pass.  "He found the body. He's pretty shaken up, but we've asked him to stay in case you wished to speak with him."

"Thank you, I do."

**20**

A few degrees cooler than outside, the church stank of aged wood and damp. She walked sombrely down the centre aisle, taking in the simplicity with which it had been built. She resisted the temptation to run her hands along the wood of the old pews.

A frail-looking, grey-haired man turned to face her, his eyes red and puffed. She could see an untouched cup of tea on the pew next to him.

"Hello, I'm Yvonne. Yvonne Giles," she said softly. "This must have been a shock..." This had to be the understatement of the year. Words seemed so inadequate at times like this.

"Yes, I can't believe it. I just can't believe it." A sharp intake of breath shook his slight frame. "Twenty years I've been warden here. Twenty years. This is a quiet village. This kind of thing doesn't happen here."

Yvonne took out her note pad. "I'm sorry, and I know this is a difficult time, but would you mind telling me your name?" She wanted to reach out to him, comfort him somehow, but remained where she was.

"I'm sorry." He rubbed his eyes. "Richard Harris, church warden. You know, he had no enemies..."

"Did you see anything unusual, over the last few weeks? Strangers around? Strange vehicles coming and going, perhaps?"

"We often have strangers here. The church is a tourist attraction."

"It is in an incredible position here, on the cliff top." Yvonne nodded. "Tell me about the church."

"In its current form, it's been here since the eleventh century. These days, we only have one or two sermons a month here. Most services are held at the new church, in the village."

"Is that the village of Llwyngwril?" Yvonne hoped she'd pronounced it correctly.

"Yes. Both churches are dedicated to St. Celynnin. There's more to the attraction here than just the position on the cliff top." His eyes narrowed, the muscles in his face tightening. She raised her eyebrows, tapping her pen repeatedly against her lips.

He continued, "Abram Wood, former King of the Welsh gypsies, is buried here. The church itself almost fell into the sea a few years ago – the west wall was splitting away from the nave. During the restoration, we uncovered some important medieval murals."

"How was the restoration funded?"

"Lottery money. Thank the lord for the Heritage Lottery Fund...see this?" The warden led her to the gable end closest to the church entrance, to a mural, the sight of which made her shiver.

It depicted a skeleton, holding a scythe in one hand and a spade in the other. Most of the skull had been lost to time. At the feet of the figure, lay a pile of bones and, to his left, the words, 'Memento Mori'.

"We uncovered this Tudor inscription when we removed some of the lime plaster. It dates from the time of the 'Black Death'.

"Memento Mori," Yvonne read.

"It means, 'remember you will die' ".

Yvonne knew very well what it meant, and felt a cold ripple peel down her back. "How big is the congregation, Mr Harris?"

"Around thirty or so regulars...there was an earlier structure here – dating from the seventh century, believed to be made of stone and wood. This truly is an ancient site."

Yvonne was curious about him. He clearly wanted her to know the history of the place. She noted this in her pocket book before closing it. "Mr Harris, I'm sorry for your loss. If you think of anything else which might help, I want you to contact me." She passed him her card.

He placed it in his pocket, "I will Inspector."

Yvonne and Dewi watched the pathologist at work.

"How did he die?" Yvonne eventually asked.

"I haven't quite finished." Hanson adjusted his gloves. "However, a bullet through the throat would be considered fatal. The exit wound is here in the side of the neck. Most of the neck muscle and part of the back of the skull are gone. The trajectory was easy to determine." He pointed to the board at the side of the room, and a diagram which demonstrated the bullet track.

"So the shooter was above the victim?"

"I'd say he was. I believe the reverend was bending down at the time he was shot."

"The killer was most likely up on the road somewhere, or in the bushes just on the other side of the wall." Dewi scratched his head, deep in thought.

"Ballistics have a bullet, recovered from the church wall." Yvonne read from her notes.

"Yes, and if I were a betting man, judging by the entry and exit wounds, I'd say this was probably the work of a sighted rifle." Hanson looked up from the body. "High powered."

Yvonne nodded. "What about the other mutilations?"

"A crudely cut cross and the words, 'memento mori'."

"Just like David Evans."

"Exactly so. There's something else..."

"Go on."

"His mouth was stuffed with seaweed."

"Seaweed?"

"His mouth was probably open when he died. The killer stuffed it with seaweed and closed it again."

"Why on earth would he do that?"

"Your guess is as good as mine. Also, the man's jacket pockets contained pasties. Three in each pocket."

"Put there by the killer, I'm assuming..."

"Well, who walks around with six pies loose in their pocket?"

Yvonne flushed. "Quite..."

**FIVE**

The rusted Victorian gate squealed and stuttered, as the Reverend Peter Griffiths opened it for himself and Reverend Meirwen Ellis. Their way was hampered by weeds and saplings, growing their destructive way between the paving-stones leading to the Presbyterian church.

The arched oak door led into a beautiful building, though water damage and years of neglect had taken their toll. The ceiling had collapsed in several places, and the rubble lay where it had fallen on aisles and pews, alike.

"The building is pretty much unusable now." Reverend Griffiths stepped gingerly over the flotsam. "It's owned by a local businessman. We are only here with his permission."

"It's a shame for such a building to crumble. Can it not be saved for some purpose?" Meirwen perused the damage.

"No." The reply was emphatic. "The front of the building is coming away from the main structure and the owner cannot afford to put it right. The intention is to bulldoze it." He spat the last words and Meirwen's eyes shot to his face. He didn't notice, taking her by the arm and leading her back outside, steadying her as she negotiated the rubble. "I wanted you to see the reality of what is happening to the church in Wales."

"Meirwen grimaced. "There's no money..."

25

"It's more than that, Meirwen!  There's no respect!  Look at this..."  He swung his right arm in the direction of the grounds. Meirwen followed the sweep with her eyes.

Next to the door, an amber-coloured plaque, dated 13th August 1875, held the name of the famous Welsh entrepreneur David Davies. To the side of the church, were piled blue plastic bags of rubbish. Vandals had smashed several of the stained, leaded windows,  and cans and crisp packets were everywhere.

Peter kicked one of the blue bags, sending it skidding across the courtyard.   Meirwen jumped, unused to seeing such anger in a colleague of the cloth. She could see him muttering under his breath and felt for him.   Here was a poignant reminder of the decline of their profession, and of spiritualism in general.  Meirwen didn't feel anger, only the wistfulness which came with defeat, an acceptance of the way of things.

She put a gentle hand on his shoulder and felt him stiffen, as though resisting an urge to shrug off the touch.  He looked down at his feet, before turning to face her, attempting a smile.  The muscles in his rugged face remained tense.

"Over there."  He pointed across the road.   "That was the main parish church of St. David's.  Look at it...trees growing out of the tower. One of our own has been murdered and his life's work is owned by an entertainment company."

"Let's go," she said, now way too uncomfortable to continue this tour with him.

"I'm sorry," he sighed. "I get carried away...David didn't deserve to die like that. It was probably thieves after the lead off the roof. That's what it's come to. Life is cheap."

All the energy and fire had left him. He stood staring at the ground, one hand on the back of his neck. Meirwen gently took his elbow and led him back to the gate. "I miss him, too," she whispered.

Desperate screams rent the air, scattering birds in every direction. Mrs Jones dropped the pile of newspapers onto her shop counter, in the village of Abbey Cwm Hir, and looked outside. A young girl ran as though for her life, her spaniel running with her, dragging its leash.

"Get the police! Please, get the police!"

"What's happened?" Mrs Jones grabbed Tina Pugh by the shoulders, her heart pummelling her rib cage.

"There's a dead man by the stones. He's got no head."

Mrs Jones steadied herself before saying as calmly as she could. "Get inside the shop, *bach*. We'll ring the police from in there."

**SIX**

When Yvonne and Dewi arrived at the village, local uniform were already questioning the girl. Yvonne grabbed a plastic suit from the van and approached the body.

There was so much blood, Yvonne put her hand to her mouth to suppress her gag reflex. Beside the body, a Labrador lay crying, its head on the dead man's chest. It was necessary to remove the animal, but Yvonne felt bad about doing so.

"I'll take that for you, ma'am." The constable had with him a lead, and proceeded to leash the dog.

Yvonne shuddered. "Thank you. Did they find the head?"

"No, ma'am, not yet."

She glanced up at the overcast sky, as it began to drizzle. In front of her was what remained of the once proud abbey – now little more than twenty or thirty foundation stones with tiny portions of wall. Yet another picturesque location had been chosen as a backdrop for the horror unleashed by the killer. The ruins, in a deep valley, were not easily accessed. The only approach was through fields, via a mud and stone track from the village.

"Whoever did this knew his way around these parts." Dewi's expression was grave as he approached. "The victim was the vicar of the local church of St. Mary. Reverend David Davies. The dog is his." Dewi checked his notebook. "Name's Bounder."

28

Yvonne closed her eyes. "We have ourselves a serial killer."

"It certainly looks that way."

"Don't say anything to the press. Not until the briefing. The DCI will have a fit."

"Right you are."

He filled his lungs with the damp morning air, sweet and earthy after the night's rain. He held his breath for a few moments before easing it out through pursed lips. The grass was soft and mossy.

He adjusted his glove and faced the brick wall, closing his eyes and lunging forward. When he opened them again, he noted the position of the point of his foil. This continued for some time, with each lunge choosing a different brick; coming at it from a different angle; aiming at blemishes on the bricks. He smiled with satisfaction. Not bad for self-taught.

**SEVEN**

The room was unusually quiet, considering it was full of CID officers. Yvonne left her seat as they waited for DCI Llewelyn to join them. Dewi glanced through his notepad, while she examined the death scene photos on the board.

The DCI walked brusquely through the door, plopping a pile of papers down on the desk next to Yvonne.

"We've got one hell of a mess on our hands." He ran his fingers through hair already well-ruffled. "I've had the bishops of both the St. Asaph and the Swansea and Brecon diocese on the phone, asking me what protection I can put in place for the clergy. We have limited manpower, but we've got to sort some level of protection for these people. As for the killer, what reason might someone have for murdering vicars?"

Yvonne cleared her throat. "Failure to become one him or herself?"

"Maybe...any other ideas?"

Dewi spoke, as though reading from his notebook. "A psychotic atheist?"

A voice from the back of the room offered. "Someone cheesed off they can't shop after 4pm on a Sunday!" What followed was a nervous laughter, which died when the DCI failed to join in.

"Seriously." He placed three pins into the map on the wall. "Three murders inside of three weeks. I want to know who wanted these men dead and why? DI Giles, what do we know so far?"

Yvonne ran her hands along her trouser legs before taking the floor. "The victims, all in their fifties, were well known rectors in their local areas. David Evans appeared to have been a well-liked, placid widower with no known enemies. He retired a few years ago due to ill health. He was later diagnosed with Alzheimer's. George Jones and David Davies, similarly, well liked by their congregations and villagers in general. On the face of it, the motive would appear to be religious, but it's important to keep an open mind."

Yvonne chalked on the blackboard. "MEMENTO MORI - that's what he etched into the skin of his victims. It means remember you will die. This is his message. What's his point? Why the use of Latin?" She paused, glancing at each and every face in front of her. "The first victim was killed with a plank of wood and then mutilated. The second victim was shot, then mutilated, he was found with seaweed stuffed in his mouth and pies in his pockets. The third victim was decapitated and then mutilated. If this is the same killer, he is varying both his MO and parts of his signature."

As Yvonne returned to her seat, she could see once again the distressed dog, curled up on his owner's body at Abbey Cwm hir.

The DCI rose to his feet. "Ask around: locals, bar tenders, church staff. Any theories, no matter how strange they may sound, write them down. Explore every avenue. No stone unturned. I want to know what weapons he used. Get everything you can from the pathologist." He turned then to the DI. "Yvonne, I'll see you in my office directly after this briefing. Everyone else, talk to whoever you need to in the local police areas to get the information we need, and I want boots on the ground and knocking on doors."

She could delay no longer. Meetings with the DCI still made her nervous, even after three months with the new force. Taking a deep breath, she gave his door a sharp rap.

"Come in." The voice was firm, definitely that of a man in command. He looked up from his papers immediately she entered the room. "Yvonne, take a seat."

She approached his large desk and sat down. To her surprise, he rose from his position and pulled his seat up next to her, notes in hand.

"I want you to take the lead in this investigation." His voice was quiet and soft, not what she was expecting.

"Yes...yes of course."

"In the station."

"Sir?"

"Out there..." He gestured towards the open window. "I'm in charge. I will be the public face of the inquiry."

She felt her colour rising. She cleared her throat, as though to protest, but said only. "Yes, sir." Her clipped tone was the only signal that she was irritated, frustration welling inside her. So, he wanted her to do all the work while he received the kudos.

His gaze searched her face before his eyes met hers. She could see he was reading her thoughts. Her eyes shifted beyond him, to his office window and the fields outside.

"Yvonne..."

She turned her eyes back to his face, suddenly self-conscious as he studied the scar on her chin.

"Not so very long ago, you were kidnapped by a violent psychopath who, I have no doubt, had been following you in the media. I will not allow that to happen again..." Now it was her turn to search his face, guilty that perhaps she had misread his motives. "...on my patch."

So *that* was it. It would reflect badly on him, should she mess up. "Well, we wouldn't want *that*, sir, would we?"

His sigh made it clear that her sarcasm was not lost on him, and she couldn't help feeling a little satisfaction at the disappointment she saw in his face.

He looked down at the notes in front of him. "I'm coming with you when you visit the murder sites in future, Yvonne." He looked up and his eyes pierced her. His voice was one of command once more. "There will be reporters everywhere and I will do the talking. Understood?"

"Sir."

"Good. I'll be giving the press conference, later."

"Can I go now, sir?"

"Call me Chris...yes, you can go."

Her chair clunked backwards. He rose with her, to hold the door open. She did her best to glide gracefully through it without looking at him.

Afterwards, she felt foolish. It didn't matter to her who talked to the press. What rankled was her being viewed as vulnerable, something she had striven so hard to leave behind.

Dewi downed the dregs of his tea just as his telephone rang. "Dewi Hughes." He glanced at his watch, his tummy rumbling.

"Hi, it's Stacey at front desk, I'm putting through a call from a Dr. Thomas."

Dewi ran his hand through tousled hair. "Sure, thanks... Hello?"

The voice on the other end was male, with a North-Wales accent. "Hello, my name is Dr. Rhys Thomas. I'm a historian with the University of Wales."

"Hello, Dr. Thomas. What can I do for you?"

"I was wondering whether you might like my help with your investigation into the vicar muders." The voice was hesitant, as though the caller were wrestling self-doubt.

Dewi grabbed his notebook. "Go on..."

"I specialise in medieval history, and I read in my local paper that the killer left inscriptions on his victims which included the Latin, 'memento mori'. That means remember you will die, you know."

"Yes, Dr. Thomas, we know what it means."

The caller cleared his throat. "I think these murders are parodies of historical ones because of the sites the killer chose and the inscriptions."

"You may be right, Dr. Thomas, but while the investigation is at a very early stage, we're keeping an open mind. I tell you what, I'll take down your details and speak to the DI and she can decide whether you may be able to help us."

Dewi sensed the caller puffing his chest out as he gave his full name and number.

"Thank you for calling us, Dr. Thomas. We'll be in touch."

Dewi shrugged as he replaced his handset. Every murder investigation had its hangers on. Armchair detectives. He found it annoying, especially when it delayed him having lunch. He took a large bite from his ham and mustard sandwich.

Reverend Meirwen Ellis adjusted her white, chasuble vestment. The material was thick and warm and she was appreciative of that. The air held a distinct chill, signalling the approach of Autumn. She was tired, and the preparation of today's sermon had been difficult. She lacked sleep and felt on edge. Almost every colleague she'd spoken to was scared, but one of the murders had been virtually on her doorstep.

She lifted her long white preaching scarf with its gold crosses on each end, placing it around her neck. Studying herself in the vestry's full-length mirror, she could see the bags under her eyes and the strain etched in her face. She closed those eyes, squeezing them tightly for a couple of seconds, breathing deep to calm herself. She was as ready as she was going to be, to face the village congregation in Nantmel, only a few short miles from Abbey-Cwm-Hir. They needed her more than ever, and she mustn't let them down.

"Are you okay?" Her verger stood in the doorway, concern in his kindly face.

"Yes, Jim. I'm okay, Well...as I'll ever be."

Jim placed a friendly hand on her arm. "It's going to be all right, Meirwen," he said softly, giving her a reassuring smile. "It's going to be all right."

## EIGHT

Newtown CID had gathered in the main, open-plan office. A cheer went up as DC Halliwell entered, unaware of the piece of paper stuck to his back, reading "Just Escaped!" He was grinning from ear to ear, but Yvonne sensed in him a sadness at the prospect of early retirement, age fifty-four. The impromptu office party had been organised by Dewi, and Yvonne had picked up several bottles of white and red from the local supermarket. There would be a toast for all those officers no longer on duty.

She began pouring into plastic cups stolen from the office water dispenser, just as DCI Llewelyn arrived. She spilled some of the wine and cursed under her breath.

"Yvonne." The DCI nodded, as he strode over to her. After mopping up the spills, she handed him a cup of white.

"Thank you," he said, studying her face.

"You're welcome. It's sad to see the DC leaving."

"Yes, he's given a lot to the service. I'm sure he'll keep in touch."

Yvonne took a gulp of her wine as her colleagues approached to take their share. She barely knew Halliwell, in all honesty, but he was hard-working and one of several officers being pensioned-off due to the latest round of government cuts. It didn't sit well. Cuts in resources were the last thing needed when hunting a serial killer.

She watched her detective sergeant as he slapped his outgoing colleague on the back. He had an easy confidence with colleagues and superiors, alike. She wished she could say the same about herself.

He was seated at the back of St. Cynllo's. The church was full, as he had known it would be, for the festival of the Eucharist. The reverend was late. Duly noted. The congregation chatted in low voices, while he stared at the door. When Meirwen Ellis finally entered, it was obvious she was tired and tense, and he knew why.

Meirwen's husky voice filled the room. "Before we begin this celebration of the Eucharist, I would like us to remember, this day, our beloved friend Reverend David Davies who was, so cruelly, taken from us. Let us give thanks for having known him and for all that he did for this parish. We will start with two minutes' silence."

He didn't want to be here for the silence, but chose not to draw attention to himself by leaving the room. He had seen all he needed, but would wait until later, as everyone stood to sing the first hymn, before slipping out of the church and into the graveyard.

He found the gravestone quickly, the cryptic carvings and lack of name confirming it was the one. From his holdall he withdrew a plastic bag. Pulling on his gloves, he removed a bloodied white collar and placed it at the foot of the stone. It had begun to smell bad, and he held his breath as he pulled away. He wished he could be here, when they discovered it, but that would be too risky. As he left, he could hear the sheep in the field and feel the peace of the place. When he had finished here, those bleats would be replaced by screams.

## NINE

Yvonne pulled into the car park of the tiny hospital in Llanidloes. She was late and cross with herself, having already cancelled the appointment twice this month. Another cancellation, they said, and she'd be crossed off the list. They explained she was lucky they still had outpatient facilities in Llanidloes: the hospital was under constant threat of closure. She rubbed her scar. It was sore and tight, pulling when she ate, and tightening painfully when she smiled. Her physiotherapy was long overdue.

The nurse sent her to the small waiting area in the corridor, just inside the entrance. She read the various leaflets pinned on the notice board and flicked through a couple of magazines. Her thoughts turned to the priest killer.

She felt jinxed, as though evil had followed her from Oxford. She felt tainted by it; could taste the bitter tang of blood in her mouth, just as she had when her jaw was broken by the sadist. If she didn't know he was still resident in maximum security, she would have feared that he had followed her here. As it was, the guilt she felt at the tragedy befalling her new home was baseless.

"Yvonne Giles."

Yvonne came to her senses, and her eyes met those of the female physiotherapist. "Yes." She rose from her seat and followed her into a small room, packed with more equipment than it was designed to hold.

She sat as instructed and waited for discomfort.

The clear gel was cold on her jaw, but soon heated up when the probe began massaging.

"This will loosen it up for you." The physiotherapist was cheery as she pressed hard with the probe, moving it around. "Ultrasound is very effective, but you must exercise your jaw, as has been explained to you. Pulling faces is a necessary evil." Her torturer smiled and Yvonne winced, as the probe hit a particularly sore part.

When the session was finished, Yvonne rubbed her scar and grimaced. "Thank you."

"You're welcome. Now don't forget to exercise."

"I won't."

DCI Llewelyn had a face like cumulonimbus, as Yvonne got out of her car. He said nothing when she approached and gave her apologies.

Finally, he motioned her over to his black Astra. "Get in." He threw open the passenger door.

"Where are we going?" she asked, throwing her handbag into the footwell.

"Nantmel. We're going to join the forensic team there. A bloodstained, clerical collar has been discovered in the churchyard."

"Oh no, not another victim..."

"I hope not." His lips were a stern line, as the engine whirred into life.

They said little on the way to Nantmel. His driving was fast but competent, and the DI felt safe enough. She opened and closed her mouth, taking the chance to flex her jaw, as instructed by the nurse. He glanced at her and she stopped flexing. He said nothing, but thought she caught a knowing look in his eyes.

SOCO and uniform were already at work in the the circular churchyard. The press had gathered outside of the church gate and Meirwen Ellis was inside. DCI Llewelyn walked over to the reporters and cameras. The hand he placed in the small of Yvonne's back indicated to her that he expected her to head on into the church, and this she duly did.

She found a hunched figure, sat in a pew, her head resting on her hands.

"Reverend Ellis?"

"Yes." The small-framed reverend was clearly shaken up. "Please, call me Meirwen."

"DI Yvonne Giles...err...Yvonne."

"Am I on the hit list?" Meirwen's eyes were very large in her ashen face.

Yvonne took hold of the reverend's cold hands. "I don't know," she answered, truthfully. "We'll assign protection to you for the time being. There will be officers with you at all times until we know what we are dealing with."

"Thank you."

"Did you notice anything unusual during your sermon this morning? Anyone you didn't recognise?"

"No, but then I was a bit distracted...you know...after Reverend Davies..."

She didn't need to say anymore, the DI slowly blinked both eyes in affirmation.

"Have you noticed anyone hanging around the area over the last week or two? Anyone walking around the churchyard?"

"I'm sorry, no." Meirwen thought for a moment before adding, "but, the church was very full today – a good turn out for the Eucharist."

"Is that usual?"

"Numbers vary, and when the church is full its hard to say how many strangers there are, especially when your mind wanders..."

"That is assuming whoever left the collar *is* a stranger."

Meirwen shuddered. "I hope it's nobody close to us."

"May I look around?"

"Of course."

43

"Thank you." Yvonne cast her eyes over the pews, the altar and the pulpit. The light entering the windows picked out the tiny particles of floating dust, sending a myriad coloured rays down into the space. A fitting place for God, she thought.

When DCI Llewelyn joined her, he appeared dishevelled. He clearly hadn't had a good time with the press.

"That's odd..." Meirwen picked one of the bibles from a pew at the back of the room.

"What is?" Yvonne rushed to where the Reverend was standing.

"This bible, it's been vandalised."

Yvonne studied the faded, leather book in question. 'FE GODWN NI ETO', had been scrawled on the front. A symbol had been roughly drawn next to the words: it resembled two crossed sickles dissected by a spear.

"Is this graffiti new?" Yvonne took a pair of latex gloves from her bag, to properly examine and bag the book.

"It must be," Meirwen nodded emphatically. We regularly check the bibles and I've never seen this before."

"What does it mean?" Yvonne asked, recognising the words as Welsh.

"It's the slogan and symbol of the FWA – the Free Wales Army." Meirwen frowned. "They haven't been active since the nineties. 'Fe Godwn ni eto' means 'we will rise again'."

"Do you know any Welsh nationalists, reverend?" DCI Llewelyn took his hands out of his pockets, to examine the bagged book.

"No, I don't." Meirwen shook her head.

"Once the bible has been photographed, and SOCO have checked around, we'll take it for forensic examination." Yvonne closed her notebook.

"Yes, of course."

"Thank you, Meirwen, for your time. You'll be assigned protection. Here is my card, for if you need to speak to me, or if you think of anything else."

Meirwen took the card, her expression taut, as she turned to leave. The DCI followed Yvonne out of the church.

He fired up the engine. "You're quiet." It sounded like an accusation.

"Am I?" Her thought-train broken, she turned her gaze on the DCI.

His eyes remained forward. "You haven't said a word since we left Nantmel. Are you annoyed at me for asking questions in the church?"

"Why would I be annoyed?"

"You might think I'm interfering in your investigation."

Yvonne shrugged. "Yes, I might."

"I'm a police officer, Yvonne. I can't just turn that off."

"Actually," she said, cutting across him. "I was thinking about her."

"Who? The reverend?"

"Yes. I think the killer may be someone she knows."

45

The DCI threw her a quizzical look. "Who?"

"She said she hadn't noticed anyone out of place at her sermon. Now, I know she said that she was distracted, because of the murders, but I walked around that church. I went up into the pulpit. Every position, every face would have been visible to her. A new face would have stood out. Would have pricked her subconscious, distraction or no."

"Someone other than the killer may have left the graffiti."

"I know, but I think it highly likely he did it and disguised his writing using capitals. My intuition is telling me this is a lone killer, and the slogan is a red herring, but I'll find out what I can about the Free Wales Army."

## TEN

On their return to the station, Dewi was calmly collating all the information on the main board: adding photographs and drawing arrows, cross-linking all of the elements he could.

"Good work, Dewi." She smiled at her sergeant. "I'll make good use of that, later."

Dewi rewarded her with a big grin. "Thanks. I need to speak to you actually, 'bout a guy who called earlier..."

"Oh yeah?"

"Historian, apparently, said his name was Rhys Thomas. Said he could help us explain the killer's messages."

Yvonne pursed her lips. "Thank you, Dewi. Get him in. We'll talk to him."

"Tell me about the nightmares." Dr Rainer, the occupational health psychologist, rested her chin on her hands and waited patiently for an answer.

Yvonne sighed, here under duress. This was just one of many psych sessions she'd agreed to, to be allowed back to work. She didn't feel she needed any more sessions, but she *was* suffering from nightmares.

"Do any involve the sadist?" Rainer prompted.

She shook her head. Her gaze moved to the window behind, it was raining hard. Her eyes glazed over, hazing the streaks of water running down the glass. "I dream of tornadoes. A lot."

"Tornadoes?"

"They always start as large, black clouds, moving in fast. Then they begin spinning and developing spirals which eventually touch down. I know they are coming for me and the people I care about. I'm filled with dread."

"What happens then?"

"Sometimes, I wake up at that point."

"What happens when you don't wake up?"

"I'm lifted up and carried over fields, over cliffs, or over water."

"And how do you feel at that point?"

"The strange thing is I almost like the fact I'm flying, and I can see a long way. I can see everything."

"And then?"

"I'm too high up. Far, far too high. I know that when the tornado has finished with me, I'm going to fall a very long way. I know I'm going to die."

"You mentioned the tornadoes coming for people you care about."

**48**

"Sometimes, I'm not the one under threat. I know it's coming for my family, or friends, and I'm frantic, trying to get them to go to safety. I'm running to warn them. Those are the most terrifying dreams."

"What about frequency?"

Yvonne shook her head.

"Are the nightmares becoming less frequent?"

"No. I don't know. I was having nightmares long before the sadist."

"After David?"

Yvonne's eyes became shiny, betraying tears only barely held back. "Yes." She swallowed hard.

"You've been on your own for quite a while. It's not a bad thing, you know, to reach out to others. Do you think you've been closing yourself off?"

"Yes...no...I don't know, maybe."

"And now you have a new case. A new killer."

"Yes."

"Are you really ready for that?"

Yvonne snorted. "Don't worry, doctor, I'm being given the kid gloves treatment." Her brow furrowed and she breathed out through her mouth.

"DCI Llewelyn?"

"He's watching my every move."

"You can understand why?"

Yvonne felt raw. She knew she'd been churlisht, recently. Rainer could see into her, and she found the scrutiny uncomfortable. The doctor was always too close to the mark. She glanced at the clock, her signal to Rainer she wanted the session to end.

"I'd like to see you again in three weeks." The psychologist's voice was firm.

"Yes, doctor." The DI said, all the while wondering how she would get out of it.

Her colleagues awaited her return. The bustle in the room died down as everyone turned to face the front. Yvonne stood by the board, prepped by Dewi.

"I don't have to tell you how serious this situation is. Three murders inside of a month, and the killer is taunting us with trophies from the victims." Yvonne's eyes sought every other pair of eyes in the room. "Dewi has kindly set out a map of events and listed the main characters on the board. Study it. I've put up a list of things we urgently need to know. He's going to kill again. He knows it. We know it. We have to stop him.

"Three victims, all priests: one killed with blunt trauma to the head, another shot, and the other beheaded. All were mutilated. The obvious link is religion, but does anything else link these men? Second, the methods used have been changing, and parts of the signature altered. Why?"

Yvonne paused, tapping her pen on her chin. "We have possible links to the 'Free Wales Army', thought to have been inactive for twenty years. Find out if there's been other, recent, nationalist activity - anywhere around Wales."

Yvonne was aware of DCI Llewelyn, at the back of the room, and made a conscious effort to slow down her speech. "Anyone have any thoughts?"

"I don't buy the Free Wales Army link, ma'am." Dewi folded his arms, leaning back against his desk. "It's just not how they operated, even when they were active. Murder was just not their thing."

"I'm inclined to agree, Dewi." Yvonne nodded her answer. "Perhaps we have a loner  who is trying to disguise that fact – trying to sound more powerful than he actually is. At face value, he has a grudge against the church but, there again, we need to be aware of the wider picture as we move forward. Keep your minds open."

"I'll be speaking to seniors," the DI continued. "We may need other expertise. I worked with an excellent psychologist on my last case. She could be of benefit."

Christopher Llewelyn frowned,  and Yvonne required his permission. She cleared her throat and shifted her weight from one foot to the other, she should have spoken to him first. In these times of recession, police budgets were diminishing and consultant fees amplifying.

51

She continued, "you'll be working in pairs, questioning villagers and sifting through the lives of the victims. We should have the full forensic and ballistic picture sometime in the next few days, but we can't wait around in the meantime. We have uniform providing protection for the reverend at Nantmel. Find out what you can about her. Who are her associates? Was, or is, she an intended victim? If not, why not? Get out and about amongst other local churches in the area. What's been happening in the ecclesiastical world? Any significant events? Any major changes to the way the church is run in Wales? We need a motive, and that means knowing a great deal more about the victims. Any questions?"

Several heads shook in unison around the room. Everyone keen to get on with it.


"Yvonne, can I have a word?"

She'd been expecting this, but it still made her stomach clench. She followed the DCI to his room.

He didn't waste any time. "Don't you think it would have been wise to speak to me before mentioning your psychologist friend?" He eyed her expectantly.

"I'm sorry, sir, I guess I got carried away." She looked down at her shoes and sighed.

"I'm not saying it's not a good idea, I just don't know that I can stretch the budget that far."

He was considering it then. Yvonne looked up at him in hope.

"I'll make inquiries, Yvonne."

"Thank you, sir."  She was genuinely grateful and her face lit up, giving her a very youthful air.  "Thank you."

## ELEVEN

A more serene and picturesque valley, Yvonne couldn't imagine. The abbey ruins, situated off the beaten track, were almost perfectly enclosed by the rolling hills. Very little remained of what must have once been an impressive structure. Destroyed during Henry VIII's dissolution of the monasteries, only small parts of the walls remained and, then, only between one and five stone courses in each section.

Wandering around, she could easily have been walking amongst the freshly pounded ruins - there being no other indication of the time period she was in.

She strolled over to the small lake, which would have held the Cistercian brothers' fish, and tried to picture David Davies walking his dog. This was the same route he had taken for many years. Where would the killer have hidden? Did he hide, or did he casually walk up to his victim prior to the killing? Did he engage him in conversation? She could imagine the reverend would have been trusting and unsuspecting. Easy prey.

At one end of the ruins, she found a long, slate stone, carved with a sword in a circle. It was dedicated to Llewelyn Ap Gruffudd - last Prince of Wales. She knelt to run her hands over the stone. Why here? Why kill in this place? This was not a church, like the two previous victim locations. Why was David Davies killed here and not at his church just down the road?

"Peaceful, isn't it?"

Yvonne swung round in the direction of the voice, heart thudding.

"I'm sorry?" She could feel dampness in the palms of her hands and clasped them behind her back, taking a deep breath. She felt very much alone.

"Rhys Thomas. I'm carrying out research in the area. I'm a historian, specialising in Welsh history."

"I see. And what brings you here?" Yvonne swallowed, now realising this was the person who'd telephoned the station, and had spoken to Dewi. A man who'd already attempted to inject himself into the investigation.

"I'm trying to track down the final resting place of the last Prince of Wales."

His tone was matter-of-fact, but his eyes did not leave her face, and she was sure that she hadn't seen him blink. Though she felt alone and exposed, she decided to use this opportunity to know more about this man, even while knowing the DCI would be extremely displeased if he found out. She was here alone, on her day off.

"Is he here, then?" She cast her eyes towards the slate commemorative stone.

"Allegedly. His headless body was carried here after he was decapitated by English soldiers at Cilmery, near Builth Wells."

He had her full attention, her narrowed eyes studyng his face.

He smiled. "No one really knows if his body is truly here. That slate stone is a modern addition. If his remains are in these grounds, they've so far not been found."

The DI's mind was whirling. The last Prince of Wales was reputedly decapitated and  buried in these grounds. Reverend David Davies was decapitated. She thought about the victim at Llwyngwril, found with pies in his pocket. Was that also related to a  historical event? She wanted to ask this lean, long-nosed historian but held back. He'd made himself a suspect and she didn't want him to know who she was, just yet. She needed to think about this - needed to talk to run her thoughts past her detective sergeant.

"Surely, you need an archaeologist if you are looking for remains?" she asked instead.

"Ahh, but I'm not looking for remains." His smile was somewhat patronising.  "I'm looking for pointers. Clues. You see, I believe that the men who buried him would have left some indication for those in the know – men of their kind, who followed in the future."

"Here?"

"Perhaps, but more likely somewhere in the vicinity.  Not too close, but not too far away.  What they wouldn't have wanted was their enemies deciphering the clues."

"I see."

"And what brings you here? Sorry, I don't know your name." He raised his right eyebrow.

"I'm visiting the area." It was only a partial lie. "And I was told this was a beautiful spot." There was no way Yvonne was going to tell him who she was and get his guard up. And put herself at risk.

"It is that. I wish I'd brought food with me. It's a great place to picnic. Well, I'll bid you good day."

As she said goodbye, she had an irrational fear he might already know who she was. She shrugged off the ridiculous thought and walked on.

**TWELVE**

Yvonne leaned back against the wall of the toilet cubicle. She felt as though her brain was bouncing around in her skull. The pain was intense. Her heart thudded as she pushed her palms against the cubicle sides, struggling to breathe.

She'd been better in recent times. The panic attacks had reduced in frequency, but this one had a vice-like grip and threatened to shake her fragile confidence to the core. Last night's nightmare was full of mutilated bodies, begging her to help them.

Footsteps approached. Firm footsteps. Confident footsteps. She closed her eyes and pushed her palms harder against the walls, to steady herself, drawing in and exhaling two deep breaths. Her eyes still tight shut, she left the cubicle.

On opening them, two shiny brown ones looked back.

"Tasha!"

"The very same." Tasha grinned. It was happiness and relief she detected in the DI's voice. The psychologist had noticed Yvonne shaking as she left the toilet, and she gave her a gentle hug. "Panic attack?"

"Yes. I'm so glad you're here. But how? What?" Yvonne inquired, as she'd heard nothing from Llewelyn, regarding whether he'd contacted Thames Valley.

"Your DCI phoned us. He told me what had been going on here and asked if I could help. Told me I'd be assisting you." Tasha grinned again, but there was also a question in her eyes and Yvonne knew she was being scrutinised. "Don't psych me," her eyes narrowed, but there was a half-smile. "I'm already being psyched enough."

"Coerced?"

"Yes."

"I see..."

"Has someone showed you around?"

"Not yet, I only just got here and I need the toilet...long journey."

"Oh, yes, of course." Yvonne stepped out of the cubicle. "I'll see you later."

"Indeed you will," Tasha winked.


In fact, Yvonne didn't see Tasha again for a few days. DCI Llewelyn had commandeered her, swiftly followed by the weekend.

"So, how are you settling in?" A smiling Yvonne poked her head around the door of Tasha's small room, at the end of the corridor.

"I'm getting there." Tasha's smile matched the DI's. "Some of us were working yesterday while others were having a relaxing Sunday."

"Working here?"

"Yes, here. Going over all the material the DCI gave me. Getting a feel for the victims and the perp. The faster I get a feel for them, the faster I give you the profile. The bodies are stacking up."

59

"I know...well I was kind of working, too, but don't tell the DCI."
Yvonne winked.    "I was pouring over forensic reports and doing the same as you, I guess, trying to get into the minds of the victims and their killer."

"And?"

"I'll tell you later, I need your advice."

"Intriguing..."

"We have so much to catch up on, how about I buy you a coffee?"

"Deal."

'The Bank' tea room was situated just off Newtown town centre. Yvonne had chosen it because the alcoves in the Tudor building offered more privacy for brainstorming and it was peaceful, away from the station.

"So, how are you now?  I mean, how are you *really*?" Tasha eyed the scar on Yvonne's chin.

"I'm fine, Tasha. A few bad dreams and the occasional flashback, but honestly? I'm okay."

"It can't be easy investigating another serial murder case so soon. It's only been a few months..."

"Four-and-a-bit months."

"Right, four-and-a-bit months."

"Tasha, I'm being treated with kid gloves. He - the DCI - is on my tail, constantly. He decided he would be the public face of this investigation, whilst I do all the work."

"Well, you can surely understand why?"

"It's frustrating. And I know that's churlish of me, but he just swans in, takes over, and gets in the way."

"Gets in the way?"

"Well...oh, never mind. I'm the one with the issues. It's not really his fault. More important, right now, is your take on this case."

"Well, you clearly have a killer who is varying both his MO and part of his signature. I think that's significant, and my feeling is that he wants someone to work out *why* that's significant."

"I think I know what he's trying to do, but please continue."

"Well, I suspect we're dealing with an individual who, on the face of it, has a grudge against the church. But the changeable parts of the signature are pointing to something else...a wider agenda. Religion is probably only a part of this."

"Could it be a terrorist group?"

"I'm not ruling it out, but I consider it unlikely. Freedom fighters tend to make demands, and rarely do they commit such personal murders, on relative unknowns."

"Right."

"I see him as a loner with a lot of time on his hands - time to fantasize and plan these murders with a fair amount of precision. Each murder telling a story."

"I found out something the other day. I revisited one of the murder sites." Yvonne sipped one of the lattés, freshly delivered to their table.

"Alone?"

"Yes."

"I thought DCI Llewelyn said..."

"Oh, I see...told you already, did he?" Yvonne sighed. "Well, I was on a day off and fancied a day out."

Tasha giggled. "You're so naughty. Seriously though, you really could be playing with fire."

"I went to Abbey Cwm hir."

"Mmmmm... The site of victim number three? What did you find?"

"A historian doing some research there. He said the remains of Llewelyn Ap Gruffudd, the last Prince of Wales, are buried there, somewhere."

"And?"

"Prince Llewelyn was decapitated."

Tasha's face betrayed the penny dropping. "Just like our third victim. So we have a copycat murderer, mimicking historical murders."

"That's my suspicion. I think the signature variations may be dictated by which murders he's depicting. I have a lot of digging to do...obviously."

"Who was this historian?"

"Well, that's something I wanted to run past you. His name is Rhys Thomas. He's an academic, but I'm suspicious of him."

"Why?"

"Dewi told me Rhys had telephoned the station, a few days before, offering his help with the investigation."

"Did you tell him you were a police officer, when you saw him at the Abbey?" Tasha leaned towards the DI.

"No."

"Thank God." Tasha sat back again.

"But he'll find out soon enough, if we take him up on his offer of help."

"Well, I would say that he must be pretty high on your list of suspects..."

"He is, but pretending he's on board could be a good way to check him out, or, if he isn't involved, get some potentially useful information. If he's our killer, he could trap himself."

"Slow down, Yvonne. We need to think this through and talk to your DCI. You'll have to admit your little jaunt to the Abbey and be prepared for a telling off. Letting in this historian could be dangerous, and we've been in this situation before."

"What about you, anyway?" Yvonne asked, a little too quickly.

"Me?"

"You. What's happening in *your* life?"

"Where do I start? I took a few weeks leave after the sadist case, then I was right back into the fray with a serial rapist profile for the Met."

"Catch him?"

"Yes, eventually.  Ten days ago he was picked up at his local supermarket, doing his shopping.  Total fluke."

Yvonne laughed.  "I guess rapists need to shop, too."

"And I've started dating..."

"Really?"

"Early days, but she's nice. Her name is Kelly and we met in a bar in Soho.  She's a high-flying business woman.  A CEO of a diagnostics company."

"Well, congratulations,"  Yvonne said, and meant it.

"Thank you."  Tasha smiled, but Yvonne felt those brown eyes searching her face.

When they arrived back at the station, people were huddled round Dewi's desk.

"What is it?"  Yvonne  asked Dewi.  "What's going on?"

"Ma'am."   Dewi leaned back in his chair, as the others drew back for Yvonne and Tasha to join them. "A small shard of metal was found in the chest of the third victim and we've just had the forensic results back."

"That's fantastic!  Does that mean we know the sort of knife used?"

"Yes, but it's not a knife. It's been positively identified as part of a fencing blade."

"Wow."

"They know the grade and blend of metals used and they're running a trace so they can identify the manufacturer and, hopefully, even the dealer."

"A fencing blade..." Yvonne frowned, as she pondered this new avenue. "Dewi, I don't know a huge amount about fencing, but I know that fencing blades are not usually sharp."

"No, ma'am. The shard was examined under a microscope and multiple striations were visible. It appears that someone sharpened the metal."

"So, we have a fencer, or someone who has access to fencing weapons. Find out everything you can about fencing: the type of weapons and other gear; clubs or societies in the Dyfed-Powys area; memberships of those clubs; and any fencers who are also members of, or associates of, the clergy."

"Right on it, ma'am."

## THIRTEEN

Reverend Peter Griffiths straightened his back, filling his lungs before launching into his seminar. The venue he had chosen was Newtown High. A large, Victorian school which had once been the local grammar school. It was now the regional comprehensive. Yvonne sat quietly in the back row of the assembly hall. It was 7.30 pm.

Her attention had been grabbed by the seminar's title, 'The Decline Of The Church In Wales'. She'd spat coffee everywhere in excitement when she saw it advertised in the County Times, wondering if the killer might attend. Her lack of credible suspects was galling, and this would at least give her an insight into the workings of the church.

Eighty to one hundred people sat at ground level. The speaker was seated on the stage at the front, flanked by two other vicars, including Meirwen Ellis. The DI sat near the back and felt safe from recognition. All lights were on the stage.

Meirwen sat to the left of Reverend Griffiths. Yvonne sensed that she wasn't entirely comfortable there.

Reverend Griffiths was striding the stage. "The Church in Wales has been abandoned, our churches left to rot and fall derelict. This impacts our jobs, families and homes. The government and councils have left the buildings to their fate. Historical buildings vandalised, their grounds used as rubbish dumps."

He gesticulated wildly, occasionally spraying his audience with spittle as he railed about the selling off of church property, especially for what *he saw* as 'peanuts'. He fixed others with his stare, daring them to disagree. She was even more interested in him.

The occasional dissenter was shouted down by the majority in the room. This was clearly an emotive subject. The killer might be here. Could be any one of these people. Might even be a member of the cloth. Her eyes travelled back to Peter Griffiths. Was he a fencer? His verbal cut and thrusts reminded her of one. She determined to set her team a-digging.

Yvonne head throbbed and a sore throat threatened. She hadn't slept well, the evening's seminar had whirled round and round her mind all night. She grabbed coffee from the machine, before going in search of Dewi, to ask him about the forensic results.

The DCI was in early, she could see him through his office door window. She wasn't prepared to see the person he had with him. Her jaw nearly hit the floor. She ducked back, but was too late.

The DCI opened his door. "Ahh, Yvonne. Just the person I wanted to see. Come in, will you?"

*Oh hell...* "Yes, sir."

"DI Yvonne Giles, meet Dr. Rhys Thomas. Dr. Thomas is a historian with the University of Wales."

"Yes, sir."

"We've met." Dr. Thomas gave her an accusing look.

Yvonne felt the colour rising in her cheeks  She looked up through her lashes at the DCI.     "We met the other day, quite by chance...when I was out walking."

Dr. Thomas interjected.  "I was doing some research at Abbey Cwm hir and thinking about the recent murder committed there.  You didn't tell me you were a police officer."  He smiled coolly.  "I would have given you my thoughts."

Yvonne groaned. *This* was awkward.

DCI Llewelyn was quiet, but she could see muscles flicking in his cheek.

"*So,* you were walking at the Abbey, Yvonne..." he said, eventually, his voice deceptively soft.

Yvonne flushed. *And you've been hobnobbing with one of my suspects,* was what she wanted to say,  but, instead: "Yes, sir. I was organising my thoughts. Getting a feel for the place and putting myself in the shoes of the victim."

"I see.  Well, perhaps you can run your thoughts past *me* after you've seen Dr. Thomas out."

She smiled weakly, and with difficulty.  Turning her attention to the historian, she held out a hand, signalling him to follow. What had he discussed with the DCI? She needed to set Christopher Llewelyn straight on a few things.

Rhys Thomas' shoes click-clacked  down the corridor.  The sound reminded her of the military.

"Are you all right to find your way out from here?" she asked, leaving him at reception.

"Perfectly," he nodded.   "You should have told me you were a police officer."

The DCI was waiting in his doorway as she walked back into CID.

"Come in a minute, will you?"

Yvonne did as she was told, pulling the door closed behind her. She pressed her lips tightly together, waiting for the onslaught.

"What were you doing at the Abbey?"

"Why did you have that man in here?" *Offence as defence.*

"That *man* is my brother-in-law. Now, I ask you again, what were you doing at the Abbey?"

"Does he fence?"

"What?"

"Oh, never mind."   Yvonne sighed.   She didn't want to fight. "I was trying to get inside the mind of the victim and his murderer. I was trying to get my thoughts straight.  It was my day off."

"You disobeyed a direct instruction."

"I didn't go there publicly. I didn't go there to interview anyone. I saw Rhys Thomas and didn't tell him who I was, but now he knows, anyway."

"I should have been there with you."

"I can't hide forever."

"I'm not asking you to hide."  DCI Llewelyn's eyes bored into her.  "I'm asking you to exercise due caution."  His gaze softened. "Please..."

"Your brother-in-law is on my list of suspects. Your co-working of this case, sir, could represent a conflict of interest."

Christopher Llewelyn spluttered out a chuckle, taking the DI by surprise.  "Hardly...I very rarely see him,  and I think I'm more than capable of not discussing this case with him."

"Fine." *Well, it was worth a try.*

"What makes you think he's involved?"

"He telephoned in, offering us his help."

"Hmmm...*got* to be the murderer, then."

\        "And I found him wandering around a murder scene."

"Which just happens to be a tourist attraction and a place of historical interest. Definitely our murderer. Case closed.  Get the file to the CPS."

"Very funny."  Yvonne had to admit that, now the DCI had put it like that, she did feel a bit silly, and she hadn't known Thomas was a relation of the DCI.  She wasn't going to cross him off her list just yet, however.

Feeling frazzled, though it was still only mid-morning, she caught up with Dewi as he poured a cuppa.

"Dewi, can you make one for me too, please?"

"Coming right up.  You look done in.  Heavy night, was it?"

70

"No, Dewi, not a heavy night. I think I might just have made a complete fool of myself with the DCI...again."

"He has a lot of respect for you."

"He did have." Yvonne sighed, and her shoulders loosened. "I feel like a very naughty schoolgirl."

"There you go, that'll soon have you feeling better."

Yvonne gratefully accepted the mug of hot tea. "What have you found about out about fencing in the area?"

"Well, there are four clubs of particular interest: one at Leighton village hall; one in Llandrindod Wells; one at the University of Wales, Aberystwyth - just down the coast from Llwyngwril; and one in Shrewsbury - just over the border."

"It'll take us a while to get around all those."

"That's what I was thinking."

"And what if he isn't a member of a club? What then?" Yvonne sipped from her steaming mug.

"From what I can make out, you can't legally own fencing weapons if you're not a member of a club. Clubs keep lists of their members, and each member takes out their own personal insurance."

"What if someone wasn't a member of a club? Is it possible to buy weapons without proof of membership?"

"Apparently, weapons do trade second hand without much vetting, and it's possible to get just about anything on the net these days."

"How long would it take to get the membership lists from all of those clubs?"

"We're on it, ma'am, and we hope to have them by the end of the week."

"I'll be speaking to the DCI again, later, about the upcoming press release." Yvonne grimaced. "The local and national papers are wanting a breakthrough. I'm unsure whether to release the information about the foil fragment. On the one hand, it may ring bells with someone out there but, on the other, keeping it quiet now might give us the edge when we make an arrest."

"I don't envy you that decision."

"Tasha will have a profile for us later today or tomorrow. That'll help us sift through potential perps. I've got a feeling we are going to end up with a fair few possibles if we add the entire membership list of four fencing clubs."

"So, you worked with her before?"

"Yes, Dewi, and she's excellent." Yvonne tucked a loose hair behind her ear. "Oh, and by the way, I'd like you to go with me tomorrow to interview someone of interest...a Reverend Peter Griffiths."

"Right you are, ma'am."

The DI cleared her throat, before formally introducing Tasha to the team and giving them a little of her back-story. In truth, most of the team had already gotten acquainted with the psychologist, who had been shifting her weight from foot to foot for the last ten minutes. She took to the floor appearing confident, but Yvonne had seen the tremble in the hand that placed her papers down in front of her.

Tasha nodded her thanks to Yvonne, as everyone settled.

"I've prepared a profile which I hope will really help in your search for the priest-killer."

The room was silent.

"I would say you're looking for a male aged around thirty-five to fifty-five. The amount of time taken with the bodies, and the care and planning, suggest a good deal of confidence. Therefore, I would focus on the older part of that age group, say, forty plus. "The guy may be a loner with a great deal of time on his hands – planning, staking out, all of these things take time. This could be someone either unemployed, through a recent redundancy or illness, or someone who is, or has has been, in the employ of the church. Perhaps, close to someone employed in the church.

"I'd say he lives alone or with an elderly parent – a parent who does not worry too much about prolonged absences. He may be a disaffected member of the clergy or someone who was refused entry into the clergy. Perhaps he dropped out or failed to graduate in theology. "He'll have a history of odd behaviours and, as a consequence, will have few if any friends, and none of them particularly close. He may even have antagonised those close to him. He will, quite likely, have written letters of complaint to councillors or his MP, and there may be a previous arrest history for violent offences, or protests. He'll be a stickler for rules.

"Since he's been using a sharpened fencing foil to inflict some of the mutilations, I'd say he's very likely a fencer. He'll like this kind of physical and mental chess, but it's an odd choice of weapon to inflict mutilations. It means they're being committed at arm's length, not up close and personal, as they would be with a knife. Since a foil would be more difficult to control than a knife, there may be a reason he doesn't want to get too close to his victims. It could be that his victims are a means to an end and dispatching them is not what motivates him.

"Although crude, the mutilations are legible. This suggests someone well-used to using the weapon. It feels comfortable in his hand.

"There are historical connotations in the staging of at least one of the murders. You could explore whether that is, indeed, the pattern with all three murders. Perhaps our killer spends his time in the local library or works with books. He may have a keen interest in Welsh history. Any questions?"

As the team threw questions to the floor, Tasha answered them with ease and the DI felt proud of her, and proud of the fact that she was her friend.

Finally, Yvonne got to her feet and glanced around her team. "Please don't say anything to anyone about this profile, yet. We still have to decide how much of it to release. So keep it to yourselves until you hear otherwise, Okay?"

All murmured their assent.

After the briefing, Yvonne met with Tasha and DCI Llewelyn to discuss the profile.

"Dr. Phillips, thank you for joining us at such short notice, and thank you for your work profiling the killer. It'll really help us focus our resources." Llewelyn pursed his lips as he closed his office door behind them. "This is one of the most harrowing cases I have known in my twenty-year police career."

"This is certainly one mean mother," Tasha nodded soberly, her hands in her trouser pockets. "He's feeding on the shock and fear his crimes are creating in the community. I'm surprised he hasn't been in contact, actually. The sort of unsub who leaves his mark on dead bodies is often the sort who also taunts the police. I think it's only a matter of time before he gets in touch personally."

"I've a horrible feeling he's just getting started." Yvonne sighed heavily. "And we can only guess where he's going to strike next."

"It's our job to stop him striking."  DCI Llewelyn waited for Yvonne's eyes to meet his before continuing.  "We should get this profile out there, ASAP.  So, what do we divulge?  What do we keep back?"

Yvonne swallowed hard.  "I say we don't keep anything back regarding the killer.  The more pointers we give to the public the better at this stage. Who knows how soon he'll kill again. We leave out one of the details, and it could have been the one to strike a chord with a neighbour or relative."

"I'm inclined to agree with Yvonne."  Tasha leaned back in her chair, rubbing her chin. "The profile's power is in how the whole thing knits together.  The more pointers, the more chance of an accurate identification."

"What about fencing?  Can we keep that detail back in case of false confessions?"  DCI Llewelyn was again looking at the DI.

"I say not, sir, I think it's a key part of the profile and the one likely to really hit home with a neighbour or colleague.  There may be fellow fencers out there who can give us a name."

"You're both agreed on this?"  The DCI looked from one to the other.

"Yes," they said in unison.

"OK, give me one detail we hold back."

"The 'rite of consecration' text that was found with the body of David Evans,"  Yvonne offered.

"That's it,  then.  Let's get more details to the press."

The drizzle invaded his hair, clouded his eyelashes, and pooled at the end of his nose. He'd spent more than an hour watching the big country house. The lights were on and the curtains open.

He watched as the other man worked in the kitchen, on the last chores before bed. At times, it appeared as though the victim was looking back at him, but he knew better. He was invisible out here, in the moonless, cloud-covered night.

He ran his tongue through the sweat on his upper lip, just as his intended victim opened the back door to take out the rubbish.

Keeping his eye to the scope, he centred his quarry, breathing in through his nose and out through his mouth. In through his nose and out through his mouth. Still. Lungs empty. Heart rate nice and slow.

'Thwip'.

As the bullet connected, his victim looked stunned. A direct shot between the eyes, spatter ballooning out from the back of his head, onto the porch behind.

He watched the lifeless body fall to the ground, grabbed his holdall, and walked over to where it lay. There would be no cross this time, just the words, 'Memento Mori' and one other word: 'Touche'.

## FOURTEEN

Yvonne caught up with DCI Llewelyn in the corridor. She was breathing heavily after running up two flights of stairs.

"Ah, there you are, sir."

"Yvonne, problem?"

"No, well, not exactly. Okay, Yes."

He laughed. "You're making perfect sense, DI Giles..."

"Sorry, I have a psych session later today and I really don't want to go. I've come to ask you if I can knock them on the head." She screwed her eyes up, as though expecting him to shout.

"Get yourself to that session," was his firm reply.

"But, sir..."

"Yvonne, you were almost killed by a psychopath, and you are currently helping to hunt down another one. I want you to finish your counselling."

"I'm fine...honestly, please."

"Okay."

"Sir?" Yvonne did a double-take.

"Call me Chris, and you can cease the sessions, but only if I take you off the priest-killer case."

"No way...you can't take me off the case..."

"Then get yourself to counselling. Now."

Yvonne closed the door with a bang and Tasha jumped.

"That man..." Frustration dripped thickly from the DI.

"God." Tasha pressed a hand to her chest. "You startled me. Who's upset you?"

"The DCI. Who else?"

"What's he done now?"

"He's forcing me to continue with that bloody counselling course!"

"Is that all? He's doing it for the right reasons. I happen to agree with him."

"He said he'd take me off the case if I don't go. I'm not so sure it's for my benefit. He's a...he's a control freak. Does he feel threatened by a woman? Is that why he's single?"

Tasha looked distinctly uncomfortable. Yvonne followed Tasha's eyes toward the door. Christopher Llewelyn's tall figure filled the frame. He turned his face away and ducked back, but not before she'd witnessed what was in his eyes – pain - he clearly hadn't wanted them to see.

Yvonne's stomach muscles clenched tight. She'd chosen the wrong moment to let off steam. She hadn't meant those words and was filled with remorse. Had she reminded him of something? Of someone?

She didn't have time to dwell. Dewi was shouting from down the hall. Their killer had struck again.

A breathless Yvonne pulled on a plastic suit and over-shoes. Dread soaking every part of her. Another victim, and they'd been unable to stop it.

The victim's house was a large, red brick, country residence, with a gated approach road. She could see dried blood on the step, bloodied drag marks up into the house, and inside the hall: blood and brain spatter smeared on the walls. The stench of death was overwhelming.

He lay about five feet into the hallway. His body had been left, arms outstretched, feet together – cross-shaped. His clothes had been ripped open, in order for the mutilations to take place. Yvonne placed her hand over her mouth, as she wretched, just managing to get outside before bringing up her stomach contents, in the general direction of an outside drain. A member of the SOCO team gave her a knowing look.

"He was found by his cleaner. She's in a state." Dewi checked his notepad.

"Where is she now?"

"She's with a WPC. "

"Who was he, Dewi?"

"A local businessman. Name of...Griff Roberts."

"Not a vicar, then?"

"No, ma'am."

"Well, we either have ourselves a copycat killer, or the priest-killer's deviating from his usual pattern. If it is a deviation, why the change?"

The DCI approached down the hallway. "They've found items which I think significant." The words were directed at Yvonne, the tone brusque.

The DI coloured. "What items, sir?"

"Fencing mask, protective kit and fencing weapons." The DCI scratched his head. "Close your mouth DI Giles."

"Did the killer leave his kit here?"

"Doesn't look like it, Yvonne. In the dead man's wallet we found a membership card for British Fencing and a business card for Leighton Fencing Club. Looks like he was a fencer."

"Our offender profile became public two days ago." Yvonne's soulful eyes met those of the DCI, as the penny dropped. "This man died because of *our* profile..."

"You think he was a fencing buddy of the killer?"

"It's a possibility, isn't it?"

"Yes...yes, it's possible."

"He's silenced him." Yvonne held her hand to her forehead.

"Yvonne, we won't always be able to second guess this killer. Even if what you're suspecting is true, we couldn't have anticipated this happening. We included those details in good faith."

"Yes, but you went with *my* decision. You would not have disclosed it if I hadn't pressed."

"Don't beat yourself up, Yvonne. You didn't kill this man. A crazed lunatic did. End of."

Yvonne gave a heart-felt sigh. "Sir...Chris, about earlier...I'm sorry. What I said, it was inexcusable. I was unfair and mean. I had no right to cast aspersions about your private life. I don't know what got into me."

"Yvonne, we'll talk about it another time." He looked weary. "Right now, we have another murder to investigate. This case needs your attention, not me."

"I know." Yvonne nodded slowly. "But I am sorry."

She gave two soft raps on Dr Rainer's door. Someone, with their mouth full, shouted, "Come in!"

She pushed the door ajar and caught the psychiatrist with a half eaten sandwich, chewing rapidly and brushing herself free of stray crumbs.

"Sorry." Rainer swallowed the last little bit. "You were late, I'd begun to think you weren't coming and so I started my lunch." She pulled a face.

Yvonne laughed as she saw the human side of the her. "I'm sorry I'm late. It's been mad in the station today." Yvonne decided not to tell Rainer that she very nearly *hadn't* come.

"How have you been over the last few weeks?"

"I've been having fewer nightmares, though they're still vivid. One panic attack last week."

"What was the trigger for the panic attack? Anything you could put your finger on?"

"Nothing specific."

"Sleeping any better?"

"Some nights, I sleep right through. Others not. It's unpredictable."

"You're suffering from post-traumatic stress. It's still relatively early days. Have you thought any more about the sedatives I offered you?"

"Yes."

"And?"

"And I think this time I will accept them. I owe it to this case, my colleagues, and the victims of this murderer, to be the best I can be. That means getting proper rest."

"Great." Dr. Rainer wrote out the prescription, "Now, tell me about David..."

Tasha waited outside Rainer's office for the session to finish.

"Oh my." Yvonne grinned. "Two psychologists in one day. I don't know if I can cope."

Tasha pushed her shoulder. "Go on with you. I came to see how you were, after being forced to continue with the psych sessions and, most especially, after the latest bad news."

"Well, to be honest, Tasha, I'm beginning to believe that perhaps I *do* need the sessions. I've been irritable, and I've been making iffy decisions, and this might just sort me out" Yvonne sighed. "As for the murder of the businessman, I can't help feeling a little responsible."

"Well, don't."

"I think Griff Roberts was killed because he knew the murderer. He knew he was a fencer."

"I've been thinking the same thing...err, not that you are in any way responsible for his death," Tasha added hastily. "But that he may have been able to identify the killer."

"I'll speak to the DCI, as I think we need to pay a little visit to Leighton Fencing Club, and he'll want to go with me. Meanwhile." Yvonne cocked her head to one side, looking thoughtfully at Tasha. "I think you and I should visit the National Library. The Abbey murder may have been based on a historical event and I'm curious about aspects of the other murders, particularly the bizarre placing of pies, in George Jones' pockets."

"My thoughts are with yours on that. The library is as good a place as any, to start with."

"And Google..."

Tasha grinned. "Library and Google, here we come."

Leighton Fencing Club was run in the village hall every Wednesday night. Yvonne and the DCI arrived at the club, looking for the organiser - an experienced fencer, Phil Hughes.

**84**

He was busy, giving instruction to newcomers, and didn't notice them at first. Yvonne took the chance to gaze around the hall, at the other fencers in the room. Some were clearly well trained and wearing full kit, others were in tracksuit bottoms. There seemed to be a fair range of ages, both male and female. To the left hand side of the hall, a small kitchen provided the chance for drinks and a chat, and a few of the youngsters were in there. Yvonne could see them through a serving hatch, running hands through their damp, flattened hair.

Phil finally caught sight of the officers, and came over, his face grave. He was out of breath. "You're the detectives?" He checked over Yvonne's ID, then continued, "We've had reporters in this evening. We almost cancelled this session. I'm Phil. I run the club, along with my wife."

"You know why we're here..." Yvonne began.

"Yes. Of course."

"How well did you know Griff?"

"Pretty well. He'd been coming to the club for three years, since he moved to the area."

"How did he seem to you, over the last few weeks? Was he worried at all?"

"No. Not that I noticed. He is always...*was* always quite cheerful. Optimistic, I'd say."

"Did he discuss any concerns regarding his business or homelife?"

85

"Not that I recall. I mean, he would occasionally talk about his business, you know, but nothing untoward that I remember. Not that we were that close. I mean, we didn't see him outside of the club...except at Christmas, for our club meal."

"Did he have regular fencing partners?"

"Everyone here would have fenced with him on a reasonably regular basis."

"Any fencers here  business associates of his?"

"Not that I'm aware of, no."

"Did he fence with anyone outside of the club?"

"A month or two ago, he requested permission to use the hall for what he called a 'personal match'.  Someone out of area.  If that's relevant."

"Did he name his opponent?"

"No. I'm afraid he didn't."

"Had he ever had a personal match before?"

"A couple of times.  He was a good fencer, and we trusted him to clean and lock up after."

"Do you have a list of members, Phil?" the DCI chimed in.   "If you have, I'd like to see it.  Also, names of members who've left, especially over the last five years, if that's possible."

"We have the current membership in our ledger, it's over there, on the table in the corner.  My wife is there, she'll show you.  The ledger goes back a couple of years. My wife will know if we've kept previous ledgers."

Yvonne took a swift step back, as a couple of fencers, completely focused on each other, battled a little too close for comfort. She headed towards Phil's wife.

"Hi."   Mrs. Hughes looked tired.   "I'm Anne."

Yvonne explained why they were there and Anne readily obliged, showing them the membership ledger.

"Can we borrow this?"

"I'm not sure... we need to have it for insurance purposes," Anne hesitated.

"We'll get it back to you as soon as we can, I promise."

"Before the next session?"

"Before the next session." Yvonne looked directly into Anne's eyes. "I'm sorry for your loss."

Anne nodded appreciation.

"Did you notice anything unusual about Griff, over the last few weeks?"

"No, nothing."

A teenager approached Anne, requiring help with the connectors on his jacket.

Yvonne turned her gaze to the rest of the fencers, paying particular attention to any who took their masks off. Perhaps their killer was among them.

Ledger in hand, she thanked Phil and Anne. The DCI accompanied her out of the hall. A rogue photographer snapped them walking out into the car park. DCI Llewelyn scowled as he pushed the DI swiftly, and unceremoniously, into the passenger side of the car. He fired up the engine and swiftly drove through the gates, out onto the main road, the photographer still snapping behind them.

"Sorry if I was a little rough back there, Yvonne." He looked across at her, as she straightened herself out, before returning his eyes to the road ahead. "I was only thinking of your protection."

"Well, remind me not to get in your way if you ever want to hurt me." Yvonne was only half joking.

Yvonne could probably have circumvented the process of becoming a 'reader of the National Library of Wales', as would usually be expected, to access its material. She was, after all, a police detective on a mission, and that probably had its advantages. However, she decided to keep her status quiet and put in a formal application.

She accompanied Tasha up the steps, in front of the giant-pillared facade, taking in the majesty of the building and its Art Deco and Greek Classical style. Elevated above the coastal, university town of Aberystwyth, it boasted sweeping views over the town, sea and countryside.

They spent hours putting in search terms, reading through summaries and narrowing lists. They hoped what they had left would be a list of the most useful books and documents.

They were told, by the helpful lady in reception, that the documents required could not be borrowed from the library but could be read in the South Reading Room. They would generally have to pre-order what they wanted.

The South Reading Room had a light, modern, spacious feel. This contrasted with the earlier 20th Century outer shell, but still felt appropriate. This was where archives, maps, photographs, microfiche and microfilm could be accessed. There were around thirty PC terminals for browsing the on-line catalogue.

Yvonne ordered historical documents for Llwyngwril, especially concerning the old church of Llangelynnin, and documents concerning St. David's church in Newtown. She and Tasha worked separately, accessing microfiche news articles. It wasn't proving as easy as they'd thought. Two hours later, they were beginning to wonder if they'd had a wasted trip.

About to get a coffee from the library cafe, they were approached by a lean figure in tweed, his dark hair had an over-comb which barely disguised his thinning hair. He gazed with interest at the books they were holding.

"Can I help you?" Yvonne pulled the books to her chest.

"No, I don't think so." His voice was thin, with a higher pitch than they might have expected. "Thank you."

Curious, she continued.   "We're doing some research...Welsh history."

He hesitated, as though cautious about conversing.   Two expectant faces were on him though.   He gave weak smile,   "I'm researching local Welsh legends and stories, for a book I'm writing."

"How interesting.  Are you an author? How long have you been doing that? What's your name?"
He wasn't smiling and his eyelids were half-closed. "Yes.  About a year and Arfon Matthews."

"Hmmmmm.   Doesn't ring a bell.   Which stories are you interested in?  We're also researching local legend, of a sort."

"Actually, you might be able to help us," Tasha joined in, and she and the DI exchanged a knowing glance - this could save them some time.

Arfon's shoulders broadened and his eyes opened fully.   "Well, I could try.  What are you researching?"

"We're looking into local churches.  There are some fascinating histories to them."

"I see."   He eyed them thoughtfully.    "Any churches, in particular?"

"I love the old church at Llangelynnin."   Yvonne smiled.   "Do you know anything about it? Or Llwyngwril village?"

"You're reporters, aren't you?"  He pursed his lips  "Looking for a back-story for the place of the murder, eh?"

Tasha and the DI exchanged glances again.  Yvonne sighed. "You've rumbled us.  Were we that obvious?"

"Yes."

Yvonne turned, as though to leave.

"There's a lot of rich history there," he said quickly. "The whole coastline was used by wreckers. Many a ship perished on the rocks because of what they did. Those sailors who were not bashed on the rocks had their heads caved in by the wreckers with mattocks and stones. Many families lost sons and fathers as a result. They say that Cornish cutters were often the target. There's a place called smugglers cove just down from Aberdovey."

Yvonne was struck by the emotion in his voice. She wondered if any of his ancestors had been affected.

"God, that's awful," she said, feeling her way. "Were any of the sailors found with pies in their pockets?" She flicked her eyes towards Tasha, who was quiet beside her.

He looked taken aback. "No, but I believe many of the Cornish cutters had pasties as part of their cargo. It was said by the locals that a sentinel now guards the area, he lies beneath an engraved stone - 'Er cof, am ogof, A dial dof' – In memory of a cave, I shall wreak revenge.'"

His audience wide-eyed, he continued, "It is said that if the wreckers return, the guardian will rise 'O'r hallt a'r helli' – from salt and brine. Look up the 'Dydd' newspaper of Dolgellau and 'The West Briton' paper of Truro, on the microfiche here at the library. Look up the death of a Mr Trelawney. I think you will find it interesting. It was said he was found with his mouth stuffed with sea weed and his pockets full of pies."

With that he was gone, leaving Yvonne and Tasha staring at each other in astonishment.

Two hot mochas later, they were hard at work looking up the death of Mr Trelawney. After some digging, they found the references.

Tasha summarised aloud for Yvonne. "Trelawney had been staying at Garthangharad Inn, where the landlord had reported him missing three days before his body was found in a cave below the cliff. The doctor and magistrate ruled that Mr Trelawney had lost his footing, falling to his death.

"The body showed no signs of water immersion. It was found in the cave, on a cairn of old bones, in a manner suggestive of some sort of ritual. Even in death, he looked terrified."

Yvonne's eyes shone with excitement. "Bingo! Tasha, our killer is aware of this story. Somehow, this is linked to our killer's motivation. Question is, how and why?"

"The microfiche articles are from periodicals here in the library." Tasha frowned "I know they have a non-lending policy, but it would be great to have more time to read these documents."

Yvonne nodded. "Come on, we can inquire."

At reception, Yvonne decided to pull rank.

"I'm Detective Inspector Yvonne Giles, and this is Dr. Natasha Phillips," she said, brandishing her ID. "We're investigating the murder of George Jones at Llangelynnin. We've found documents that may be of significance, and we're wondering if we might borrow these periodicals." Yvonne placed her note paper in front of the receptionist, who peered at them over her glasses, before calling over the librarian, who also checked Yvonne's ID.

"I'm sorry," the librarian said slowly. "We have a policy of not lending from this department."

"I know that, but..."

"And in any event," he continued, "the pages you refer to...in those periodicals, are missing."

"Missing?" The word was thick with disappointment

"They were stolen around six months ago. Unfortunately, thefts of old documents are not that uncommon – hence, the no lending policy."

"Who had access to them at the time they were stolen?"

"A 'Dr. Fish', who had set up his online account two days before. Local police checked the address he gave and found it to be false. The address existed, but Dr. Fish, not surprisingly, did not."

"Did you lend the books to him?"

"No. He requested them from archives and read them in the reading room."

"Did you have CCTV running?"

"We did, and Dyfed-Powys police had the tape. Dr. Fish was wearing a beany hat, large-rimmed glasses, and a long coat. The stills were grainy, and a positive identification pretty much impossible."

Yvonne raised her eyebrows. "That's eccentric clothing, did that not raise suspicions? Ring alarm bells?"

"My dear, this is a university town. This place is visited constantly by students and academics from all over. We are *used* to eccentric."

Whatever she'd been expecting, it wasn't stolen documents. Yvonne had gone from excited to deflated and, from the look on her face, Tasha was feeling no better.

"Back to the drawing board, then." Tasha sighed, as they left the building.

"Yes, unfortunately, but we've learned quite a bit, and we can get our team onto the CCTV footage from the library. What if the thief were our killer? If they can find out who accessed that reading room around the dates of the theft, we could put that together with the profile and the other information we've gathered. Just maybe we can crack this case." Yvonne flipped up the collar of her coat. It had begun to rain.

**FIFTEEN**

"Yvonne." DCI Llewelyn was waiting for her. "We're going to a fund-raising event. The bishop of St. Asaph, Dafydd Lewis, is expecting us at All Saint's church. I thought we could catch him whilst he's in the area. How you fixed?"

She was tired, and could do without going to a fund-raiser, but she fully appreciated the chance to talk to the bishop about the murders in his diocese. "Give me five minutes, and I'll be with you."

Roughly twenty people were milling around the church when they arrived. Lots of tea-drinking, biscuit munching, people examining the stalls for bargains.

The greying bishop stood near the door, talking to a town councillor about his future retirement plans. Chris Llewelyn strode over to them, Yvonne close on his heels.

"DCI Llewelyn," he announced, his voice raised in order to be heard above the general chatter. "And this is DI Giles."

"How do you do?" Yvonne shook his hand.

The councillor made his excuses and ducked away, leaving them alone with the bishop.

"Someone is killing Welsh clergy and the killer is still out there." The words were propelled at the detectives like bullets.

"I'm sorry for your losses, bishop, but he's not only killing your clergy. Two nights ago, he killed a local businessman. Do you have any idea who might be doing this?"

"You think it's an inside job? Do you suspect a man of the cloth?" The bishop ran a hand through his hair.

"Do you know anyone who might have had a grudge against David Evans?" Yvonne kept her tone calm and even. "I understand he was retired."

"I hadn't seen David since the Christmas before last. I thought him a very pleasant fellow, and I don't know of anyone bearing him a grudge. I don't think he'd ever really recovered from the loss of his wife. He was diagnosed last year with the early onset of Alzheimer's. I know of no-one who didn't like him. He was kind and gracious to all around."

"Bishop," DCI Llewelyn intervened. "When we found him, we discovered a piece of paper containing words we think would have been read at a consecration or dedication of a church. Is there a reason that the reverend would have been using it at the church, on that particular evening? The words included the name of St. David's, particularly."

Yvonne shot the DCI a questioning look. Hadn't they agreed to keep that fact quiet?

"I think it unlikely, officer. That once proud parish church has not been in use since 2006, when it was discovered that it was structurally unsafe. There was no money to fix the issues and it was sold off, around a year ago, to a private leisure company. There would have been absolutely no reason for David to be carrying out a consecration. Although, as I said, he was diagnosed last year with the beginnings of Alzheimer's disease. Maybe he thought he really *was* carrying out a consecration."

"Please don't talk to anyone about what we've just told you, Bishop." Yvonne stated.

"You know, I don't know if this may be relevant, but..."

"Yes?"

"Not long after St. David's was built in 1847, the church was consecrated by the person who was the bishop at the time, but up until around the 1940's, there was much confusion and debate about whether the church had been properly dedicated to the saint. The church was built after the original parish church, of St. Mary's, had been subject to vicious flooding, and was no longer considered fit for purpose. St. David's was the replacement.

"The first parishioners of St. David's regularly referred to it as St. Mary's." The bishop paused, as though to recollect some more. "I believe a vicar, even as late as the 1920's, was inducted into it as the church of St. Mary instead of St. David.

97

"It wasn't until 1943 that the original dedication was confirmed as having happened during the laying of the foundation stone. The bishop, of that time, then declared that it would, from then, always be known as St. David's."

"Could David Evans have been re-enacting this dedication when he was killed?"

"I don't see why he would have been doing that, Inspector."

"What if the killer were making him do it?"

"Again, I don't see why that would happen."

"What direction is the church in Wales going to take in the future, Bishop Lewis?"

"There are changes afoot, if that's what you mean. There was a meeting in July of this year about the future. I'll be retiring in a few years, I dare say the church'll look a little different by then."

"Do you regret that?"

"No, not as such. I'm tired. I'm also a little set in my ways. Change is inevitable so, when the time is right, I'll hand the baton over to someone else. Someone fit to run the diocese after all the changes."

Numerous people were awaiting the attention of the bishop, and it was with reluctance that Yvonne accepted she was out of time. She backed off, as the DCI thanked the bishop for his help. She decided she'd speak to Daffydd Lewis again, soon.

Griff Roberts lay stiff and cold on the mortuary table, his lifeless body a testament to the ruthlessness of this killer. If, as Yvonne suspected, he was a personal friend of the killer, then this murderer was prepared to kill and mutilate his friends in order to save himself from exposure. She pondered this as she entered. Roger Hanson continued his examination of the victim.

He looked up as she approached. "Good afternoon, Yvonne. This one follows the pattern we've seen previously. In all likelihood, he was killed on his front doorstep with a sighted, high-powered rifle, fitted with a silencer. The bullet struck him right between the eyes and blew away most of the back of his head. He would have known nothing about it."

"We found him in the hallway." Yvonne felt queasy and closed her eyes for a moment.

"Yes, he was dragged from where he was killed, further back into the house. He could be mutilated without fear of discovery there."

"Hmmm, dragging him back into the house would certainly have given the killer privacy and, of course, would delay the finding of the body."

"The same primary inscription was carved into his upper torso, 'Memento Mori', but here," Hanson pointed to the abdomen, "he carved the word 'Touche'."

"That's obviously a reference to fencing."

"Yep."

"I think he was killed because we released a profile, suggesting the killer is a fencer. I think the victim fenced with our perp. I think there must've been something else, though, some other fact or facts which Griff knew — something which, together with the fencing, gave the game away."

"Interesting."

"Did the killer do anything else to the body?"

"There were no other mutilations, if that's what you mean, and I can detect no other interference with the body."

"Thank you, Dr. Hanson." With a heavy heart, Yvonne took her leave of the mortuary.

The next morning, Dewi handed her a thin file when she arrived in CID.

"Ma'am, you'd better see this. Apparently, Griff Roberts was a member of a gun club. He had a full gun licence."

"Really?" She pursed her lips, digesting this new fact.

"I took the liberty of contacting the gun club and they listed the weapons he held."

"And?"

"A 9 mm handgun; a 12 bore shotgun; a 9 mm semi-automatic, and a high-powered hunting rifle."

"Where are the guns?"

"Well, all but the high-powered rifle were in a locked gun cabinet in Roberts' house."

"Where's the rifle?"

"Missing."

"Are you thinking what I'm thinking?"

"That the killer has the missing rifle?"

"Yes. Was it stolen during the murder?"

"Unlikely, the key to the cabinet was in a locked drawer, in Roberts' home office. The drawer was undisturbed."

"What if he'd lent the rifle to his killer?  It might be why the businessman was killed, before he put two and two together, following the release of our profile."

"It's certainly a possibility."

"Talk to Roberts' friends.  Someone will know something."

## SIXTEEN

The air was hot and dry, and the sunlight dazzled them, as it bounced off the sea. Tasha pushed open the gate leading to the graveyard, at the old church of Llangelynnin. They were greeted by the sweet, earthy smell of freshly strimmed grass. The grass-cutter's tools were strewn on the side of the path.

Yvonne took Tasha to an area still cordoned by blue and white police tape, and pointed towards the parking bay, up on the road, about two hundred metres above them.

"The shooter was up there, somewhere this side of the wall. He had cover from the trees and bushes on the slope. He was able to take his time and wait for the right shot."

Yvonne walked to the arched church door. "George Jones was approximately here, bending over, we think." Yvonne bent over, demonstrating his position. "And that is when he was shot. Thing is, he only gave a sermon here once a month. It was due that evening. He was only here that morning to prepare a few things."

"So, the killer either knew George and his movements very well, or he didn't know him, but had been watching him for some weeks prior to the murder."

"I agree. I suspect our killer knows the workings of the local churches, or stalks his victims for some time, before the kill. I'm worried that he is now stalking someone else."

"Have you still got protection on Reverend Ellis?"

"I have. I'm still convinced she's a target. She has asked if she can have her protection removed though, and that concerns me."

"What does the DCI think?"

"He thinks that if the murderer had wanted to kill her, he would have done so the day he left the collar in her churchyard."

"Perhaps that had been his plan."

"Well, if it was, why wait? Why not follow through?"

"Maybe he has a soft spot for her? Or maybe the opportunity just didn't present itself. There were a lot of people at her sermon that day."

"Yes, but he could have killed her before the sermon."

"Perhaps he wanted her to suffer mentally. To fear him. Savour the control over her."

"I saw her the other evening. She was at a meeting in Newtown High School. Reverend Peter Griffiths was the lead speaker. He was very vocal and, I would say, almost militant in his frustration at the decline of the church in Wales."

Tasha jerked her head in Yvonne's direction. "That's a potential motive right there..."

"Exactly what I've been thinking. I think we need to pay him a visit."

"I agree, but first, let's eat our sandwiches down there." Tasha pointed to the bottom of the graveyard, with its gorgeous view out to sea.

The vista was spectacular. They set down their flask and sandwiches atop a large, oblong monument and sat, swinging their legs in the sunshine. Yvonne felt more relaxed than she had in some time.

The skin on Peter Griffiths' face appeared fluid, in the flickering orange light, as he lit candles on one side of the altar. The church of St. Cynon was eerily quiet.

He appeared entirely focused on what he was doing, his brown grey-flecked hair looked like it hadn't been combed for a while, and this gave his thin face a wild air.

Yvonne was surprised her footfall hadn't caught his attention, as she approached along the flagstones. She stilled, silent and patient, in the middle of the church, watching and waiting for him to finish. It didn't seem right to intrude on his quiet contemplation.

"Can I help you?"

She almost jumped out of her skin. He'd said the words without turning round. He'd known she was there all along.

"I hope so," she replied with all the calm authority she could muster. "And perhaps I can help you."

She had his attention. He finished lighting the final candle, and turned to face her.

"I'm DI Giles, and I'd like to talk to you. I'm sure you're aware of what's been happening to some of your colleagues, and I've come find out if you have any concerns, or if you have any idea who might have committed the murders."

"You mean you've come to find out if I was involved."

That threw her. "Why do you say that?" She tilted her head.

"Well, isn't that why you're here, detective?" The words were ejected coolly, without emotion. It wasn't the reaction she'd expected.

"Questioning those who knew the victims is part of my job." She felt as though she were knocking a ball across a court, like the warm-up for a tennis match. Something about his demeanour unsettled her. She sensed a tension, barely held in check.

"I did know them – the victims. Aren't you worried I could be next?"

Yvonne pursed her lips in thought. "I'm concerned for every vicar in this part of Wales, yourself included."

"I feel safer already."

"How well did you know the victims?"

"They were colleagues. We talked to each other occasionally, shared the odd social event etc. Discussed current issues..."

"Were you close to any of them?"

"I wouldn't say close, no, but definitely on friendly terms."

"When did you last see them?"

"I last saw David Evans about five years ago, a year after he retired from the church. I didn't know George Jones as well at the other two. I last saw him at a Christmas gathering about eighteen months ago."

"And David Davies?"

He paused. "Four weeks ago."

"So quite recently..."

"I went to see him to ask for his support for a petition to the Assembly government."

"May I ask what the petition was about?"

"The Welsh church is in decline. Its position has been weakened and undermined by government legislature, over the last several decades."

"Go on..."

"Well, shops open on Sunday and pubs open on Sunday. God's day. People are forced to work, especially in retail, on Sunday. There's been a drying up of funding for work to save the buildings. I could go on."

"How did Reverend Davies respond to your request?"

"He thought change inevitable. That we couldn't stop progress and that, effectively, I would be wasting my time."

"How did you respond?"

"I asked him to think about it... We've seen our living standards decline dramatically. We barely have enough to live on. Not only are our church buildings crumbling, but many of the vicarages have been sold off. It's rare these days to find a vicarage actually inhabited by a vicar. We simply can't afford to run, repair, or live in them."

"Where were you on Tuesday, fourth of August?"

"You mean where was I when Reverend Davies was killed?"

"Yes."

"I was home, writing a speech for a gathering I was organising at Newtown High School."

"Can anyone verify that, Reverend Griffiths?"

"No, 'fraid not. My wife left three years ago. I live alone in my cottage next door and I didn't see anyone. I have a daughter, but she has very young children. I don't see them very often. "

"I see." Yvonne scribbled her notes.

"I heard of his death on the Wednesday morning, as I didn't watch any TV on Tuesday evening. I think you should know, detective, that I contacted his wife. I telephoned her when I heard."

"Do you know her well?"

"I don't know her at all, really. I knew of her, and I met her once some years ago, but I had David's home number and I called. I just wanted to offer my condolences and my support."

"I see. I'll be talking to her in due course. Thank you, Reverend Griffiths, for your time. I shall let you get back to your candles." She turned to leave but, after taking a couple of steps, swung back around. "If you think of anything else, please contact us."

"I will, detective." He didn't smile.

When Yvonne returned to the station, it was seven o'clock. The lights were still on in the DCI's office and she was surprised he was working so late.

She gave his door a tentative knock.

"Come in." He sounded tired.

"I saw your light on, sir." She paused in the doorway. "I came to see if you are all right."

"Yvonne..." He put down the notes he had been reading and turned his tired eyes towards her. He was a handsome man, though his hair was ragged from hand-combing. The knot of his tie was falling loose and the top couple of buttons on his shirt were undone.

"Sir..."

"Chris."

"Chris...I wanted to tell you how sorry I am, about my angry outburst. I was peeved, and the things I said were hasty and unfair. I was horrified when I saw how my words had affected you. I hadn't meant for you to overhear."

"Did you mean what you said? Do you really think I'm alone because I'm a control freak?"

"Firstly, I don't *really* think you're a control freak, and secondly, I don't pretend to know why you're alone."

"What made you so angry?"

Yvonne swallowed hard. "I feel like I'm still grappling with the legacy of the Sadist. I feel that people...you, especially...are treating me as though I'm fragile." Yvonne thought honesty the best policy. "I was angry that you wanted to be the public face of the inquiry, I thought you wanted the kudos. I wasn't prepared to think more deeply about it because I wasn't prepared to admit I might be wrong."

"I see."

"I truly am sorry, Chris."

"Would you like to know the *real* reason I'm on my own?"

"Only if you want to tell me, sir."

"I was married for fourteen happy years. We had our ups and downs, but there were many more ups than downs." His head was bent and his eyes, roving around the papers on his desk, were glazed. Yvonne knew he was seeing a different time and place. He continued. "She died two years ago."

"Oh God, I'm sorry..."

"Cancer of the throat. It was too quick. One moment, I was taking her to the doctors because she felt unwell, and the next...she was gone."

"And the house was silent and empty, and minutes felt like hours and hours like days."

"That's exactly right." He raised his head now, his eyes meeting hers, his brows raised in silent inquiry. "You, too?"

"Yes. Me, too." She smiled a sad and knowing smile. "My husband, David, passed away two years ago. He died in intensive care, following a gliding accident."

"Then I, too, am sorry," he said softly, and in that moment, they were united in something: a shared understanding of that dark part of their histories.

Yvonne stood to leave, but turned just before reaching the door. "Would you object to my talking to your brother-in-law, Chris?"

"Rhys? Don't you mean question him?"

Yvonne looked down at her shoes and shifted her feet. "Yes."

"You did tell me he's one of your suspects..."

"Well, he is..."

The DCI gave a small laugh. "Be my guest. I've never been all that fond of the fellow, anyway, but he *is* my sister's husband. Please keep me informed, as that is the one interview I will not be able to accompany you on."

"I'll keep you informed, sir."

The DI shut the door gently behind her.

Yvonne and Tasha were at the seaside and, once again, on business not pleasure. They climbed the wide, stone steps to Aberystwyth Art Centre, at the University campus, on Penglais Hill.

The campus afforded sweeping views over the town and on to the sea. The noise of gulls filled the crisp sea air. Yvonne took a long and lingering lungful.

As they reached the plateau, on the approach to the big, glass-fronted Art Centre, Yvonne's eyes travelled the full length of a tower to their right, which she decided must be modern art.

"They call it the Stanley Knife because of it's shape."

She whirled around. Dr Rhys Thomas was standing below them, at the bottom the steps. "I only just got here," he continued. "I thought I was going to be late." He appeared calm and not at all flustered. Yvonne suspected he'd been there a while.

"The journey from Newtown took *us* longer than expected. There were a lot of road works." Yvonne took in his neat suit and tie and slicked-back hair. "Thank you for agreeing to speak with us."

"I'm a bit pushed for time, actually, I was wondering what this might be about." His steel caps click-clacked with every footstep as they headed into the centre. "I'm glad you could meet me here." The words were said lightly enough, but the muscles in his face were stiff. "I'm giving a lecture and time will be tight. We could get coffee in the cafe."

Yvonne ordered the coffees: lattes for herself and Tasha, and a cappuccino, as requested by Dr. Thomas. When she took her seat, she had the view over the bay. The sun sparkled off the water in a myriad of dancing lights – fairies going for a swim, her mother had once said.

"You'll remember, Dr. Thomas, when we bumped into each other, at Abbey Cwm hir?"

"I remember." He leaned back in his chair and eyed her warily. "I was looking for clues, more ancient than the ones you seek."

"Clues to the whereabouts of the last Prince of Wales."

"You remembered."

"Do you recall telling me how the prince met his end?"

"He was run through by an English Lancer, and was identified as he was dying. He asked for a priest and was instead decapitated."

"You'd know the details as well as anyone."

"I'd hope so."

"The mutilation of the murder victim found at the abbey involved decapitation."

"I read about it in the paper, gruesome stuff."

"And you felt there might be a connection?"

"That's right. I contacted your team and asked to speak to the lead detective."

"The lead detective is DCI Llewelyn." She smiled. "So I hope I'll do. My colleague here is Tasha. She's helping us with the case."

Tasha smiled at the historian and sipped her latte, continuing to quietly observe.

Rhys Thomas nodded at Tasha, before continuing. "It struck me that the priest was slain close to the Prince's memorial stone. The decapitation struck me as a helluva coincidence."

"We're investigating several murders, all of which appear to have superficial similarities to murders in Welsh legend."

"Am I a suspect?"

"You offered to help us." Yvonne's face betrayed no emotion. "I'm very interested in your take on these crimes. We're still trying to establish motive. The victims were all mutilated, and the words 'Memento Mori' carved into each one."

"That slogan has been used throughout history, in graveyards and churches, to remind people that they should be God-fearing and attend church. If you remember death, and that you will have to justify all of your actions to God, you're more likely to be a good person whilst alive."

"Do *you* believe that?"

"I'm just outlining its historical use, Inspector. During the time of the Black Death, these murals were painted in many churches, always reminding the congregation of their mortality and the need to worship."

"Is that why you were contacting the team? To tell us that?"

"Of course. I'm married to the DCI's sister. I just wanted to help."

"How long have you been a history professor, Dr. Thomas?"

"About twelve years."

"What did you do before that?"

"Post-doctoral study. Before that, I was a student."

"Do you have any connection with the church?"

"So, I *am* a suspect...Do I need a lawyer?" His tone was facetious.

"Dr. Thomas, I can't really form a list of suspects until I've established motive."

"Oh... wow... is that the time?" He pushed his chair sharply back, the chair legs scraping the floor.

"I'm sorry?"

"I thought I'd explained, my time today is short and my lecture starts in fifteen minutes."

Yvonne sighed and shrugged.   "Dr. Thomas, thank you for your time. We'll be in touch."

She stood up as the historian turned to leave, her face betraying her disappointment.

"You'll get another chance" Tasha gave her a gentle nudge. "You're not going to avoid upsetting people when you're questioning them in connection with a string of murders.   If you ask me, he's hiding something."

"You think?"

"Don't cross him off your list."

"Oh, Tasha, we're looking for a sword-wielding, gun-toting, religious fanatic with an interest in history. You'd think he'd stand out a country mile."   She took a deep breath.   "Plus, he could be all of those things or none of those things and, even if he is all of those things, he may be all of those things without anyone knowing he is all of those things."

Tasha chuckled.   "Hey, if these cases were easy, we wouldn't need people like you to crack them. You're up to this challenge. Have faith in yourself.   Now then, Llewelyn will be waiting, so get yourself to the station and talk to the intriguing Mr. Matthews."


"So, it's you." Arfon Matthews pursed his lips and tutted loudly. "It's a bit disconcerting when you receive a request to talk with police, out of the blue. Now, I realise I've spoken to you before."

The DCI gave Yvonne a questioning look, which Yvonne ignored.

"Yes, Mr Matthews, I'm sorry I didn't introduce myself properly before. I wasn't talking to you in an official capacity."

"How can I help?" Matthews tapped his thumb on the edge of the table.

Do you remember telling me about articles in these periodicals?" Yvonne pushed a photocopy of the library lending records towards him. The periodical entries were highlighted.

"Yes, of course I do."

"Those same periodicals have missing pages. Torn out. Stolen."

"Is that why you asked to see me? Do you think I would steal items from the nation's heritage?"

"I haven't said that." Yvonne kept her expression blank.

"You must suspect it. Otherwise, why talk to me?"

"You may have ideas about who might have stolen them. When did you last access them yourself?"

"I don't know...um...a year ago?" He shrugged his shoulders. "I didn't loan them. I used the microfiche."

"Do you know anyone else who might have an interest in loaning them?"

"Not really, not those specific journals, no."

"Do you know a 'Mr. Fish'?"

"No."

"Mr Matthews, my name is DCI Llewelyn, I'm the lead investigator in a murder inquiry."

Yvonne stifled a frown.

Matthews turned his attention to him.

"You were a student in Aber, in the late seventies and early eighties."

"Yes, I was."

"You were arrested and charged, in..." David Llewelyn checked his notes. "1982, for affray."

"I wasn't convicted."

"No, that's right, you weren't, but you *were* cautioned. Members of the Free Wales Army were present. You were spending a lot of time with them, weren't you?."

"What's that got to...Look, I was young, impressionable and opinionated. I thought the FWA were exciting."

"Did you attack houses? Set any fires?" Yvonne shot at him.

"Look, Wales was officially known as a third world country back then. Many people still had outdoor toilets...drew water from wells. Hell, some houses didn't even have electricity. Mid-Wales, especially, was in decline. So much so, in fact, that the government commissioned a Mid-Wales development board to revitalise the area – attract new businesses in."

"Did you think you could make a difference?" The DCI was, again, doing the questioning.

116

"Newtown was known as the 'capital of Wales', during the woollen trade. It had been a rich town with a working network of canals. Flooding, and the decline of the woollen trade, put paid to that. People deserted in droves. What we were left with were empty shops, beautiful houses used only as second homes by holiday makers, and a language and population in decline. This was made worse, in my opinion, by the cheap, poor quality housing estates set up to house immigrant workers, populating the new factories which sprung up because of government incentives."

"Immigrants?" Yvonne interjected.

"Yes, English people. They came in to take up the work, with the promise of cheap housing. Welsh farmland was bought up and turned over to housing. There were a lot of disgruntled locals."

"Were you a member of either the Free Wales Army or Meibion Glyndwr?" Yvonne hoped she'd said the latter correctly.

"What if I had been?"

"Do you think those organisations could be rekindled?"

"The late seventies was a time of serious recession. We're in recession now. Who knows?"

"Would *you* be for rekindling them?"

"Inspector, I'm in my early fifties. My marching days are over. I leave those activities to the young. I told you, I found it exciting at the time. I wouldn't these days. Now, if I'm not under arrest, can I go?"

The DCI flicked his head. "Of course, this was just an informal chat."

117

When they arrived back in Newtown, Tasha was waiting for Yvonne, her eyes shining with excitement.

"Tasha, what's happened? You look like you're going to explode."

"I've been finding all I can on the Free Wales Army and Meibion Glyndwr. There's a mine of information about them. Also, other organisations that most of us have probably never heard of."

"I thought you saw the Free Wales Army reference as a red herring?"

"I do, inasmuch as I still believe this to be a lone individual, but that doesn't mean that our killer hasn't taken on their old beliefs. He may even hold their ideologies close to his heart."

"Okay, go for it."

"Well, the Free Wales Army, or Mudiad Amddyffin Cymru, as they are known in Welsh..."

Yvonne raised her brows and grinned, as if to say, 'show off', at Tasha's Welsh pronunciation. "Who told you how to say that?"

"What makes you think I had to be shown?"

"Tasha, nobody knows how to pronounce large Welsh words like that without being shown"

"Alright, it was Dewi."

"I knew it."

Tasha pushed out her tongue. "Anyhow, they first became public in 1965. Apparently, they were voicing protest against the flooding of a village called Capel Celyn in Gwynedd in North Wales."

"Flooding of a whole village?"

"Yes, the village was evacuated by force to allow the flooding of the valley. The construction of the Llyn Celyn resevoir, which was going to be a source of water for the people of Liverpool."

"You said *forced* evacuation..."

"The people from the village and local farms were offered money for their homes. Many accepted it, seeing that the building of the reservoir was pretty much inevitable, but many didn't. Some of the elderly residents said that they would rather die in their homes than leave. Some families had owned their homes for generations."

"So the flooding went ahead."

"Yeah. By then, everyone had been removed. There was massive opposition in Wales. The village was a stronghold for Welsh language and culture."

"I see."

"The FWA also helped the families of the Aberfan disaster, when a slag heap, from a coal mine, slid down a valley and buried a primary school. Most of the children, and their teachers, died in the tragedy. The FWA supported compensation claims for the families, as it seems that claims were being thwarted by authorities at that time.

"I had no idea the FWA had their fingers in so many pies."

"Neither did I, till I started digging."

"There were also suggested links between the FWA and the IRA, and it was reputed that the IRA sold its armaments to the FWA, when it relinquished violence, prior to 1969. They were also said to have trained FWA in military techniques over in Ireland.

"There were also suggested links with Basque separatists, but those were more difficult to pin down."

"Wow, I had no idea. What about Meibion Glyndwr?"

"Sons of Glyndwr, were Welsh nationalists. They were definitely in favour of using violence, in order to halt the loss of Welsh culture and language. They were famous for torching second homes, which had been purchased by people from England."

"Well, if what I was told by Arfon Matthews was right, then there would have been a lot of empty homes on the market, due to the large efflux of Welsh people when the woollen industry collapsed."

"Oh, I'm not sure about that. Anyway, torching the homes was the way they chose to deal with it, and this continued from around 1979 to the mid 1990s."

"I'm impressed, Tasha, you've been busy."

"Google is an amazing resource." Tasha grinned. "Just one more thing. There were a few other nationalist groups, including: Cadwyr Cymru - the keepers of Wales; and WAWR – the Welsh Army for the Workers Republic. Meibion Glyndwr was, though, the most successful. Interestingly, a Welsh MEP speculated at the time that they were a front for MI5."

"Why would MI5 use a Welsh nationalist group as a front?"

"Access to the IRA? I don't know, and I also don't know what basis he had for suggesting this, I'm afraid."

"Have you got all this down?"

"Yes." Tasha held up her pad.

"Great. Arfon Matthews, the Welsh legend researcher we met at the National Library, was associating with the FWA in the late seventies."

"Hmmm..."

"Quite."

Meirwen Ellis sighed, deeply, as she climbed out of her Mini Metro and walked towards the church at Nantmel. She gave a cursory nod to the two officers standing outside, just as she'd done to the two officers outside of her home.

She hoped resentment wasn't showing on her face. She felt guilty about feeling it. They were only doing their duty, trying to protect her. However, week on week, she had witnessed her congregation becoming smaller and smaller. Soon, she would be preaching to herself.

As she crossed the threshold of the church, a voice came over an officer's handset, startling her, and she placed a hand against her chest to calm her racing heart. She couldn't blame her congregation, everyone was nervous.

Her verger, placing the flowers at the back of the church, greeted her warmly as she entered.

"Thanks, Jim," she said, when he handed her a cup of milky coffee. "I wonder if we'll have many here today."

"It'll get better," he smiled reassuringly. "The killer will be caught and then it'll all be back to normal. You'll see."

She wished she could believe that and, later as she crossed the church to the pulpit, she counted only three expectant faces. This couldn't continue. She'd speak to DI Giles and get her to call off the protection.

"Meirwen, I can't do that."  Yvonne's brow furrowed, her voice earnest, as she spoke into the phone.  "In all conscience, I don't know where this madman is going to strike next. He's already called at your church, of that we're sure.  We have reason to suspect he may be stalking his victims for some weeks prior to harming them. We cannot guarantee that he hasn't been stalking you.  Our officers have been vigilant but I wouldn't put anything past this killer, Meirwen"

"Please remove my protection...It's what I want. It's not helping me."  Meirwen's voice was strong and firm.

"Look, I'll speak with the DCI, but if he gives his permission and we remove your protection, I want you to carry a personal alarm at all times.  We'll program the emergency number into your mobile, so it's triggered by one button. I have to tell you, in no uncertain terms, you will be in danger if we do as you request."

"You can leave the protection at my house. I am grateful for it, honestly, just please remove it form my church."

Later that day, with the DCI's permission, and against Yvonne's better judgment, the protection duty assigned to St. Cynllo's church at Nantmel, was called off.

## SEVENTEEN

Dewi scratched his head as he rummaged through the papers on his desk. Yvonne perched herself on one corner of it, swinging her legs.

"Ma'am," he said, without looking up...

"Lost something, Dewi?" she asked, as she plopped a hot mug of tea down for him.

"Oh, thank you." He eyed the tea gratefully. "Yes, I've been through the membership list of Leighton Fencing Club and identifying potential perps, according to Tasha's profile. I seem to have mislaid them..."

"You mean these?" Yvonne pulled a wodge from behind her back, one eyebrow raised.

"Oh phew." Dewi looked relieved.

"Well, what have you got?"

"Two possibles: John Rees, thirty nine years old, runs his own carpentry business. His family own a farm out near Dolfor and he has a gun licence."

"Where's Dolfor?"

"About five miles out of Newtown, on the Llandrindod Wells road."

"Does he have an interest in Welsh history?"

"Won't know until we question him, but he is fluent in Welsh."

"Okay, and who's the other one?"

"Kevin Abbott. He's thirty four years old, and a consultant cardiologist at Shrewsbury Hospital."

"How does he fit the profile?"

"Well, he lives in Bettws, a village six miles from Newtown in the Shrewsbury direction. He's married to a Welsh woman and has a gun licence. He's also a member of a gun club near Knighton.

"Well done, Dewi. We'll talk to both of them."

Meirwen had a haunted appearance, her eyes dark and hollow, her face gaunt. After the events of the last few months, she ought to feel fear, even terror. Instead, she felt calm. Numb. She told herself she was probably too tired to feel anything else.

Removing her chasuble vestment and scarf in the vestry, she examined her image in the full length mirror. Yes, it was a good job she wasn't vain, she mused.

She thought she saw a shadow pass behind her in the mirror, but shrugged it off. She'd seen a few things that weren't there recently. Her tired mind playing tricks. She walked across the room and placed her holy garments on the back of the chair. Hearing a rustling, a lump developed in her throat. She wasn't expecting anyone.

"It's you, isn't it?" She tried to sound strong, calm and steady, but the wobble in her voice betrayed her. "It's my time, isn't it...You've come for me." She didn't try to look. Didn't want to see the face of her murderer.

124

"*Do not turn around. Do not look at me.*"  He didn't know the words were unnecessary.

Expecting either no reply or a human voice, what she heard took her by surprise.  The intruder was using text-to-speech.

"What is it? What do you want?"

"*If you do as I say, no harm will come to you.*"

Meirwen bit her lip and could taste the iron tang of her own blood.  "And if I don't?"

"*I will kill you.*"

She swallowed hard and began praying silently.

"*Put this on.*"

The figure in black was behind her, handing her a cloth bag.

Although scared, there was some reassurance in his use of text-to-speech. If his intention was to kill her, there would be no need of either the device or the blindfold.

With shaking hands, she took the bag and placed it over her own head.

"*Come with me.*"

His hand on her elbow, fingers digging into her flesh, making her wince.  He pushed her roughly forward.

She felt her way along, disappointed with herself for giving up her protection. Both her mobile phone and her personal alarm were in her bag, in a cupboard in the vestry. Jim had left early, to go to a family get together.

Her foot caught a doorstop, on the way out of the church, and she tumbled, headlong, onto the path. The killer, to save himself, had let go of her and she hit her head on an iron shoe-scraper.

As she was pulled to her feet, she felt, a cold trickle of blood down the right side of her face. He shoved her in the middle of her back, propelling her along the pathway leading from the church. A car door was opened and she was forced, headlong, inside. A plastic cable tie was used to bind her wrists behind her. She heard him go around to the driver's seat and the central locking engaged.

Her breathing was hot and heavy inside the bag. In her mind, she was screaming.

Yvonne pulled up outside the three-storey house of Griff Roberts. She passed through police tape, which was still there, following the departure of SOCO and the clean-up team. She guessed that the grief-stricken partner of Griff had not had the heart to remove it, just yet.

Her heart slowed, till it was barely beating, as she gripped the brass door knocker and pounded twice.

The door was opened by a small-framed, young woman, who appeared painfully thin. Dark shadows, under red-rimmed eyes, gave her a lost look, and Yvonne's heart went out to her.

"Della?" she asked gently. "Della Roberts?"

"Yes."

"My name is Yvonne. Yvonne Giles. I'm a Detective Inspector with Dyfed-Powys police.

"Come in." Della turned her back and Yvonne closed the door behind them.

She was led into a large sitting room, which was dimmed by half-closed blinds. A half-eaten plate of food lay on the glass coffee table, along with several part-filled mugs, whose contents were beginning to separate. There were various items strewn on the floor and a pile of dirty clothes was stacked unceremoniously in the corner. An ignored tabby cat mewed underneath the coffee table.

"Shall I feed it?" Yvonne asked gently.

"Sorry?"

"Your cat."

"Oh, of course. Come into the kitchen. We can talk there...and feed Tigger."

Yvonne followed Della into a huge, black and red kitchen, ultra-sleek, with chrome fittings. Once there, she began checking the cupboards for tins of cat food, and was shocked by how little food there actually was, either for the cat or Della.

"There are sachets in that cupboard, down there." Della pointed vaguely at the corner. Yvonne found the cupboard on second go, and took a sachet of food from a box inside. The cat's bowl she located near the kitchen door. Tigger bounded up to her, rubbing himself on her knee, as she opened the sachet and ejected it's contents into a bowl, which had been licked clean. She finished off by putting fresh water in the bowl next to it. Tigger purred love in return.

127

Della, lost in her own thoughts, gave no acknowledgement.

"I'm so sorry for your loss," Yvonne began, tentatively.

Della looked in the direction of the DI, but her eyes remained unfocused.

"It must have been a shock."

"We argued...the night before he was murdered." Della gave a strangled sob. "I told him I hated him. I went to stay at my mother's h...house."

"Had he upset you?"

"We'd been arguing more and more, over the last year."

"Was there a particular reason for that?"

Della gave another sob which shook her whole frame. Her long, auburn hair fell forward and all but covered her face. "He was out a lot, and would regularly have weekends away with his friends. Some weekends I didn't get to see him at all."

"Della, can you tell me who those friends were?"

"Some of them, I really didn't know many of them. I think a few had started out as customers of his firm. Some were from the fencing club, and others from the gun club. There were some guys he'd known in school..."

Needle in a haystack sprung to mind, as Yvonne ran her hand through her hair. "Did any of his friends figure more in his life? Any he spent more time with? The weekends away, for instance, anyone in particular?"

"He didn't always tell me who he was spending time with, Inspector. He'd tell me to have my friends round, or he'd buy some tickets for a spa weekend for me and my bestie."

"Did he ever mention concerns about change in Wales, perhaps particularly in connection with religion?"

Della frowned, and looked at the DI fully for the first time since her arrival. "That's a strange question. Why do you ask that?"

"Well, as I'm sure you're aware, your husband appears to have been murdered by the same killer who killed three priests and, we think, part of the killer's motivation may be anger at what he sees as a decline in Welsh culture."

"What would my husband have to do with that? Yes, he was a Welshman, but he spoke English. Yes, he was proud of his Welsh background and yes, he enjoyed talking about Welsh Heritage but he was no fanatic. I've never heard him moan about a decline in anything. He was a lay member of the church, though."

"We believe he knew his killer."

"Oh God..."

"Your husband kept guns."

"Yes, I'm in the process of selling them."

"He had a sighted rifle, high-powered. We didn't find it when we went through his weapons. Do you know what happened to it?"

"To be honest, I didn't know what weapons he kept. He had them before he met me and, although I knew he had guns, I didn't have anything to do with them."

Della appeared like she might pass out at any moment.

"Have you eaten?" Yvonne suspected not.

"No."

"Is there something I can get you?"

"No. Thank you, officer. I will eat shortly." Della sighed when she saw the doubtful expression on the DI's face, and added, "I promise."

Meirwen felt nauseous. She wasn't sure how long the she'd lain on the back seat of the car. The twists and turns in the road had given her heartburn, and she thought she might be sick into the cloth bag around her head. Just when she thought it was imminent, the car pulled over onto a gravelled area. As it came to a halt, she began retching.

The back door was pulled sharply open and she was dragged out by her arms. Her knees scraped on the gravel, the tiny stones penetrating her skin. She felt their texture but not the sting.

She could hear the gentle lapping of water and felt a strong breeze tugging at her clothes and the bag around her head. It relieved the heat inside it.

When the bag was pulled off, she screwed her eyes up against the glare. It took a full few seconds of blinking for her to be able to properly open them.

"*Don't look at me.*" Text-to-speech was back.

Meirwen did what she was told and looked straight ahead. She was shivering, though the day was not cold. She recognised this place. To her right, were the stumps and roots of trees, exposed due to the recent hot weather. She was about to ask him why he had brought her here, when the bag was pushed back over her head and she was dragged to the water's edge.

She knew, then. Knew the fate that awaited her. Somehow, she had known all along – had been waiting for it to happen. At least it would be an end to the fear. She was almost glad. She closed her eyes in silent prayer. As she felt the cold water on her face, she lost control of her bladder. She didn't struggle.

**EIGHTEEN**

"No! No! No!"

Yvonne put her hands on either side of her head, swaying from side-to-side. Christopher Llewelyn was terrified she was about to pull out handfuls of her tousled hair. He raced over and pulled her hands away. He saw the tears in her eyes and the guilt deep within them.

"You are not responsible for this, Yvonne. This was not your doing."

"We took the protection away from the church."

"I know, and that was ultimately my decision, Yvonne. I take full responsibility for that. But you know that we cannot force protection on someone who doesn't want it."

"I should have worked harder at persuading her..."

"She was losing her congregation through fear, Yvonne. She was trying to reassure them. She was putting others first. Preaching was her vocation. Her life would have been meaningless without it and she told us some of her sermons had been delivered to a congregation of two or three. For her, that was unacceptable."

"They'll crucify us, for taking away the protection detail, and I'll deserve it."

"I'll speak to the papers. Right now, I want you to go take a break, get some coffee. If you don't feel better, I want you to go home – take a day off. Take a few days off."

"No." Yvonne gave him a stern look, shaking her head emphatically. "No time off."

"Then, go take a breather. Come back in half an hour."

It took monumental effort to hold back the tears. After leaving Llewelyn's office, she ducked into the toilets and let go: swearing, crying and grabbing at paper towels so roughly, that none came away intact.

"Meirwen, I am so sorry," she said, staring into the mirror, her mascara staining the tops of her cheeks.

Meirwen's body had been found by tourists at Llyn Celyn reservoir. She'd been drowned and mutilated. The inscription etched into her torso, all too familiar.

"They found tyre tracks in the gravel." Dewi put a gentle hand on the DI's shoulder, as they surveyed the horrific scene.

Yvonne wiped her eyes with the back of her hand. "Can they get a print?"

"They'll do the best they can, but they've already told us that it's unlikely to be anything usable for identification purposes."

"Make sure they get decent photographs. Something we can enhance. We're going to find this evil bastard and bring him to justice."

Tasha joined them, having travelled up with uniformed officers. "Yvonne, I just heard."

"Tasha, we should never have allowed the detail to be taken off the church. I knew it was a terrible idea."

"Short of whisking her off somewhere remote, under witness protection, I don't see how we could have prevented this. He would have gotten to her somehow."

"Not if she'd stayed in her house and we'd kept the officers on her church."

"That wasn't the life she wanted, Yvonne. I could see it in her eyes, she was suffering from survivor's guilt. It was almost as if she were determined to put herself in harm's way. But hey, she was expecting him, wasn't she? If I were a betting woman, I'd put money on her having found some way to leave us a clue to his identity. She was taken from the church, right?"

"Yes..."

"We'll start there. A bright woman like Meirwen will have left some sign, I'm sure of it."

Tasha always knew how to make her feel better. Yvonne was glad of her presence.

Six o'clock, and DCI Llewelyn was waiting for her outside the station. Yvonne put on her coat more slowly than usual. A feeling of dread ran through her.

They were going to interview a suspect from Leighton Fencing Club, John Rees. Yvonne knew they had to up the tempo, there were too many victims already. Local and national news reporter groups were virtually permanently camped in the station car park.

When they arrived at Leighton village hall, a lean man in his early forties was pacing up and down outside. His dark hair was partially hidden by a waxed hat, cocked at an angle, shirt sleeves were rolled up to the elbows, and his thumbs were hooked into the front pockets of his faded jeans.

"John Rees?" Yvonne asked, closing her car door.

"That's me." The answer was delivered with a gruffness.

"Thank you for agreeing to see us. We'll be as brief as we can."

His only answer was a nod.

Yvonne cleared her throat, as the DCI joined her. "I'm DI Yvonne Giles and this is DCI Christopher Llewelyn."

John Rees looked from one to the other, giving each a brief nod.

"We're investigating a series of murders in the area, including that of Griff Roberts. We have reason to believe our killer may be a fencer or have access to fencing weapons. We believe that Griff knew his killer. It's possible the murderer is a member of this club."

"Come on inside." Rees turned for the door. "I've borrowed the hall keys. We can have a cup of tea in the kitchen."

Yvonne and the DCI exchanged glances and he motioned her in before him.

They passed through the entrance hall, where photographs of various sporting actions hung on the wall, including a black and white shot of fencers sitting around, masks off, chatting and enjoying themselves. Yvonne paused, was their killer among them?

Rees led them to the kitchen, off the main hall, where he proceeded to fill a kettle.

"How well did you know Griff Roberts?" DCI Llewelyn leaned back against the counter-top, his expression thoughtful.

"Quite well. We weren't close friends but we talked now and again at club functions and shared a few jars."

"What sort of functions?"

"Christmas meals; drinks at club; birthday drinks – that sort of thing."

"Ever been to his house?" Yvonne accepted the tea offered, setting it down on the counter-top.

"No. Never."

"Had he been to yours?"

"No."

"Did you know his wife?"

Rees hesitated.  "I met her a couple of Christmas's ago. She seemed sweet."

"Did Griff own weapons?"

"I think he was a member of a gun club and had a few guns."

Yvonne's eyes narrowed at this swiftly delivered reply.

"Did you ever see his guns? Did he ever show them to you?"

"No, we really weren't that close. I think he'd have been more likely to share that sort of thing with his gun club friends, not his fencing friends."

"How did you know about his guns?"

"Occasionally, he'd mention they were having a shoot at the club. I think the shoots were mostly on Saturdays, but he didn't ever go into detail."

"Do you have an interest in guns, Mr. Rees?"

"Not at all, Inspector." His eyes pierced her, as though daring her to challenge him.

"Do you know anyone else, here at the fencing club, who does?"

"None that I know of."

"You'd tell us if you did..."

"Of course."

As they finished their tea, both Yvonne and Chris knew they would get little more from John Rees. His frequent sighs and distracted gaze said it all. As did his picking of non-existent lint from his trousers.

Yvonne took a card from her pocket. "Will you call us if you think of anything else, or you hear anything you think we should know?"

"I will. Sorry I couldn't be of more help." His face was impassive, giving Yvonne the distinct feeling he wasn't at all sorry.


As they travelled back to Newtown, Yvonne rubbed the hard ridge of her scar, deep in thought.

"Penny for them?" Llewelyn asked, keeping his eyes on the road.

"I don't know about you, but I didn't feel anything coming from him. I mean, even if he wasn't close friends with Griff, surely he would have expressed shock – hurt, maybe. Concern for Griff's wife...something, but he was emotionless."

"I know, he wasn't asking questions. He didn't ask if anyone else at the club might be at risk."

"He's just moved himself higher up my list of suspects."

Another fencer, Kevin Abbott, was waiting for them at the front desk. Dewi had signed him in and was busy making him a coffee. Kevin was only too willing to assist, and had even kept the sergeant on the phone, earlier that day.

In the interview room, he was relaxed but concerned. A tall man, he appeared a little uncomfortable when positioning his legs. Yvonne was struck by his unusually large hands, especially since she knew he must perform some very delicate operations with those hands.

"Dr. Abbott, this is an informal interview," she began. "We are trying to get as much information as we can to help us piece together the events surrounding the murder of Griff Roberts. I understand you were both members of the same fencing club?"

"It's Mr...If you're a surgeon, it's Mr. We were in the same club. Griff was a nice guy. One of the more competitive fencers at the club. Awful thing, to happen to him. Do you think his death was related to the murders that have been all over the TV and the papers?"

"Possibly," Yvonne said, thoughtfully. "How well did you know Griff?"

"Quite well. I knew him from the club, and I'd been on a few pheasant shoots with him. I didn't kill many, I wasn't very good."

"Do you own guns?"

"None of my own. I went with Griff, at his invitation. He always supplied the shotguns."

"I understand that he was also a member of a gun club. Did you ever go to this gun club with him?"

"No, I'm not that into club shooting."

"Did Griff ever express worries or doubts about anyone else at the fencing club?"

"No...I don't think so..." Kevin's eyes were closed, as he struggled to recall. "Oh...no...wait...Yes, he did, just a few weeks ago."

Yvonne leaned forward. "What did he say?"

"He said he'd been to the club on a Saturday for a practice session, for a competition which was coming up in Wrexham."

"Okay..."

"He said that he and an opponent had a really tight match."

"Go on."

"After the match, Griff took off his fencing mask and his opponent lunged forward and placed the plastic tip of his foil right between Griff's eyes."

"Why did he do that?"

"Griff didn't know, but he was certainly scared at the time. He could have had a serious eye injury."

"I'm guessing that's not how fencers normally behave."

"No, it isn't. Like I say, Griff was very shaken at the time. Afterwards, the guy just laughed it off, like it was nothing."

"Mr Abbott, who was the opponent? Did Griff tell you?"

"No, I'm afraid not, Inspector. Our chat was interrupted by a youngster wanting to practice. I meant to catch up with Griff over a cup of tea, in the kitchen afterwards, but he'd left early and that was the last time I saw him. I was working a lot of long shifts at the hospital, and didn't fence much for a few weeks after that."

"I see."

"I wish I'd asked him. I really, really wish I'd persisted in asking him who that man was. Now, at the club, I'm looking at people and wondering if it was them. Griff had only signed himself in that day. I guess he'd been expecting his guest to sign in, likewise."

"Do you have any firm suspicions about who that guest might have been. Anyone capable of such a risky gesture?"

"No, Inspector. I've not had any issues or bother with anyone at the club. Of course..." Griff continued, "there's a chance this wasn't a normal club member. We sometimes have fencers visit from other clubs, and there was a big competition coming up. This could easily have been someone from Shrewsbury, Wrexham or even further afield.    Those clubs have a lot more members than our little club at Leighton. It's not unknown for Team GB fencers to pop in, every now-and-again."

Yvonne had been afraid that Kevin would say that. They would, of course, chase up information regarding members of those other clubs, but that could take a long time, and they could end up hunting down the membership of half the clubs in Britain. This angle was beginning to look a lot  less hopeful.


After the interview, Yvonne sat down for a coffee with DCI Llewelyn.    "What do you think about the sword-between-the-eyes incident?"

"I think that could easily have been our man...it suggests arrogance and aggression.  Fits our profile."

"I agree.  I had hoped the fencing angle might narrow things down for us, sir, but it's done the opposite. Our profile may have gotten Griff Roberts killed, and it may not yield us anything." Yvonne cupped her head in her hands. She felt sick, and still couldn't forgive herself for either Griff or Meirwen's death.

St. Cynllo's, in Nantmel, was eerily silent. It seemed as though even the birds had deserted it. Yvonne waited for Tasha to catch up with her, as she entered the circular graveyard.

They had come to take a fresh look at where the killer had previously placed the bloodied collar. They'd brought with them some of the SOCO photographs, to enable them to orientate themselves.

The air was damp and cold. Yvonne's knees clicked loudly as she knelt next to the nameless tombstone. She closed her eyes. "Why is he leaving a collar, from the body of his previous kill, at the sites of his next victim?"

Tahsa considered. "I think he doesn't want to leave the door open for copycats. If we had a body without this calling card, we'd know it wasn't his work."

"Because every kill has a significance to the story he's telling..."

"Yes. He's giving us the pieces of our jigsaw, piecemeal. He *wants* us to connect the dots, but only on his terms and according to his time-line."

"I can't see anyone else wanting to copycat this."

"Me neither, but he clearly wants to be sure they don't."

"Why didn't he kill Meirwen on the day he left a collar here?"

Tasha sighed and rubbed her chin. "He may have been in two minds. Perhaps he knew her, liked her, and changed his mind last minute. Or it could just be that he was disturbed by something and fled."

Yvonne couldn't imagine this killer *fleeing* from anyone. "He wanted her to know what was going to happen – keep her terrorised."

"He was always going to pick her off at a time of his choosing. I have no doubt she was afraid, but we couldn't protect her because, for whatever reason, she didn't *really* want to be protected. Survivor guilt. I've seen it many times."

"This was supposed to ward off demons!" A strangled, male voice came from behind them.

Yvonne swung round, heart in her mouth. "Hello? Who are you?" She took her ID from her pocket. "We're from Dyfed-Powys police. I'm DI Giles and this is Dr. Phillips. We're investigating the murder of the Reverend Ellis."

The older man nodded "I know who you are." He brushed his greying hair back from his face. "I'm Jim. I'm the verger, here. You're standing in a circular churchyard. They're supposed to ward off demons but that didn't work for Meirwen."

Jim's face was drawn, dark semi-circles under his eyes. Tasha's eyes were gentle as she responded. "Demons were not responsible for Meirwen's death, Jim. A living, breathing human being was."

Yvonne had an urge to comfort him, but held back. "Tell me about the circular churchyard." Although voice was soft, her eyes were urgent as she rose from the earth. "I'd like to know more."

Jim rubbed the small of his back with both hands, as though in some pain. "These churchyards go back to ancient Celtic times, when stone circles were used to carry out religious ceremonies. They're all over Wales."

"So a stone circle would have been here, originally?"

143

"Yes. The circle of standing stones was called 'the Gorsedd' and they were used by pagans to carry out their rituals. The same circles were later adopted by the early Christians. Many churches in Wales were built on these ancient sites. The Welsh druids used the Gorsedd, and the National Eisteddfod is opened with a druid and bard's ceremony, in a stone circle, every year."

"Is there *still* pagan practice in Wales, these days?"

"There are people who practice. I don't know much about them. White witches, they sometimes call themselves."

"Do you know any?"

"No."

"Jim, when was the last time you saw Meirwen?"

"The day she died."

Tasha and Yvonne exchanged glances. Yvonne continued. "How did she seem to you?"

"Sad and scared. She hadn't been herself for weeks. I thought she was losing weight and I was worried about her. I gave all this information to the two officers who came to see me, a few days ago."

"I know, forgive us, we're just clarifying a few things. What was she doing that day?"

"She'd given a morning sermon and performed a baptism. It was a normal sort of Sunday for her."

"What time did you leave her?"

"Around two o'clock. She was going to stay awhile. She was sorting out music and hymn scores for a wedding, to be held here at the church. I didn't want to leave her alone, but she insisted. It was my daughter's twenty first birthday, you see, and myself and my wife were preparing everything for her party."

"So you left at two o'clock." Yvonne made notes. "Did she say how much longer she'd be here?"

"She said not much more than an hour."

"Did you notice anything suspicious when you left? Vehicles parked up?"

"No, not that I recall, Inspector."

"Any people around? Walkers? Cyclists?"

"No...none."

"Did Meirwen say if she was expecting anyone?"

"She said she was going to finish up at the church and go straight home. She'd left a casserole on slow cook, in her oven."

"What will happen here, now? Who looks after the congregation?"

"The vacancy will be advertised by the diocese. In the meantime, I will step up, to cover some of the sermons, to give as normal a service to the community as possible."

"Speaking of which..." A voice boomed from the other side of the churchyard.

Yvonne recognised it immediately and every muscle tightened. "Peter Griffiths," she called back. There was definitely something about him that made her uncomfortable.

**145**

He raised his eyebrows. "Do I know you? I'm sorry if I do, it's just not coming to me," he said, as he was closing the gate behind him.

"We're police." Yvonne felt perhaps she ought to be questioning Peter Griffiths under caution, but had no real basis for arrest. "I saw you talk at Newtown High school, a couple of weeks ago."

"I see." He seemed momentarily thrown, but quickly regained his composure. "I'm here to collect some of Meirwen's belongings for her family. We were friends. We'd been friends for several years."

Yvonne thought about this. Since she'd watched him, at the meeting in Newtown High School, he'd been high on her suspect list. However, Meirwen had been at the meeting, and she was supporting him in his cause. If he was the killer, why would he kill someone who supported him? Besides, his being vocal about a decline in Welsh culture was hardly a crime.

Tasha was quiet, but the DI knew she would be weighing up both the verger and Peter Griffiths. Yvonne's voice was firm, as she asked Peter Griffiths not to remove anything from the church until police had given the go ahead.

Yvonne arrived home, shattered. Throwing her bag onto the hall table, she went straight through to her kitchen and poured herself a cold glass of sauvignon blanc. After a fraught week, arriving home early was a luxury. She took her wine outside, to catch the evening sun.

The air was warmer than it had been, with the thick, sweet smell of late-summer flowers. Her view, over her low stone wall, went out for some distance - over the valley and to the hills beyond. She breathed deeply. It was good to be home.

Momentarily forgetting her troubles, she sat on the wall and looked back at her home. She loved it. It was quirky. Victorian Gothic, with interesting features everywhere she looked. It was also hard work, with almost constant maintenance. When Yvonne didn't have time to do it herself, which happened often, she would hire local lads from the village to help out. She'd decided on the house very soon after arriving in Wales and had been lucky. There was no onward chain. She felt content. Happiness had been a rarity for months, but she felt it now and wanted to hold onto it - for a little while.

"Is this a party for one or can anyone join in?" Tasha stood at the gated entrance to Yvonne's car park, with a bottle of wine and a great big grin.

Yvonne grinned back. "Well, since you've brought wine..."

"Great! What's for dinner?"

The DI laughed. "Beef tagliatta with Tuscan fries."

"Wow! I have no idea what that is, but it sounds really good."

"It will be, if you can keep me off the wine till I've cooked it."

With Yvonne in full flow, a hot pan sizzling in front of her, Tasha poured her a fresh glass of red. The smell was driving the psychologist mad. "Can I do anything?"

"Nope, got it all under control."    Yvonne took a big glug from her glass.    "Well, actually, you can lay the table, if you like."

The steak rested, Yvonne cut it into diagonal strips and scattered it onto a large plate.  Chopped tomatoes were dropped around the plate and the marinade drizzled over everything.  The Tuscan fries, she tipped into a bowl and sliced up warm ciabatta, to accompany.  Tasha looked as though she couldn't take it any longer.

Yvonne laughed at the look on her face.    "Come on, let's get stuck in."

There followed a couple minutes silence, save for the soft sound of munching.

"I'm not being ignorant," Tasha said between mouthfuls.    "This is just too damn good, for talking."

"I'm glad it's that good."

After the meal, and two glasses of wine, they retired to Yvonne's lounge.

"So, how's Kelly getting along? It must be difficult for you both, while you're down here."    Yvonne plumped herself onto the Chesterfield.

"It does take some getting used to.  She's been working very long hours as well,  and I do feel guilty being here, at times.  She understands, though. We have a killer to catch."

"Yes...this killer...I can't sleep.  I keep going over and over everything.  Almost every day, someone else is thrown into the frame.  They all have potential motive."

"I think the killer means to confuse us regarding motive. I was tempted to moot some ideas with you, this evening, but decided against it. You need your rest."

"What ideas?"

"It can wait till tomorrow."

"What ideas?"

"Well...I was doing a little homework and came across something really interesting. Could be relevant."

"Go on." Yvonne leaned towards her, elbows on the table.

"You were saying the other day, you thought the murders had historical basis and appeared to loosely copy historical events."

"Except Meirwen's murder...yes."

"Okay. You also said that the murder at Abbey Cwm hir could have been based on the death of Llewelyn Ap Gruffudd."

"Uhuh."

"I've been doing some digging. Reverend David Davies was found close to the memorial stone and he was headless, right?"

"Yes. He'd been decapitated, and we still haven't found the head, despite conducting a massive search of the whole area."

"I brought some notes with me." Tasha pulled a wad from her handbag. "The story of the prince's death changes depending on who's telling it. Although the main tales are *broadly* similar, they differ widely in the details."

"Hmmm...RhysThomas was trying to tell me that, at the Abbey when I bumped into him."

"Well, Llewelyn Ap Gruffudd had a daughter, Gwenllian. After her father was killed, in 1282, Gwenllian and Llewelyn's niece were exiled.   They were sheltered by monks, in the East of England. According to their version, Llewelyn, at the head of his army, rode out to meet the combined leaders of four English forces.  These included those of the brothers Edmund and Roger Mortimer and Hugo Le Strange. He'd been told that they were going to pay homage and join him."

"Okay..."

"It was a trap.   Llewelyn found himself in a fierce battle, in which a significant section of his army was routed. He, and around eighteen retainers, *including* men of the church, became cut off. The monks had it that the prince and his men were ambushed at dusk and chased into a wood at a place called Aberedw, near Cilmery."

"How is this related to our murder?"

"I was just getting to that bit...they cut off the prince's escape route and ran him through.  According to the monks, he didn't die straight away but called for a priest. It was this, or the way it was done, which gave him away and his enemies cut his head off. What happened to the head is a subject of controversy...but..."

"I get it, our killer may have dealt with David Davies' head in the way, he believes, the English dealt with Llewelyn's head?"

Tasha's looked excited.     "Yes. Yes, that's exactly it. What do you think?"

"I think you're onto something."

"I vote we speak to Dr Rhys Thomas again; find out what *he* thinks was the likely fate of Llewelyn Ap Gruffudd's head, in 1282."

"But, what if he's our killer?"

Tasha looked thoughtful. "Either way, I don't see how we can lose. If Rhys Thomas is our killer, I believe that he won't be able to resist giving us the true version of events, as he sees it. After all, this murderer is an exhibitionist. Every murder scene screams at you, 'Look at me, look at me, look at what I've done'. I think the killer is waiting for us to find the head."

"And if he's not the killer? We might go looking up a blind alley..."

"Maybe, but it sounds like he might be a foremost researcher on the subject, so he may still be our best bet of finding the rest of the Reverend Davies."

"Okay, agreed. Where shall we speak to him?"

"The station. If he is the killer, it'll rattle his cage."

"Or..." Yvonne rubbed her chin. "What about meeting him at the Abbey? I'd value the chance for *you* to observe him, in the place where David Davies lost his life. If he is the killer, he may give himself away."

"What would the DCI make of us doing that? Are you going to tell him?"

"Sure, there'll be two of us, and Chris can't come because of conflict of interest."

"Chris, eh?" Tasha winked. Yvonne blushed.

In the sultry heat, Yvonne and Tasha approached the ruins of Abbey Cwm hir.  The birds were in full song, but heavy, black clouds were gathering.

This was Tasha's first time at the site, and they were about twenty minutes early, so Yvonne took the opportunity to show her around.


"It's such a beautiful  place."  Tasha breathed deeply of the valley air.  "I can see why they would want to build an Abbey here. What does 'Cwm hir' mean?"

"I think it means 'Long Valley'."

"Learning Welsh, huh? I'm impressed."

"I'm trying."  Yvonne grinned at her.  "Just don't tell Dewi."

They both laughed, imagining his reaction.

"Can I share the joke, ladies?"  The voice behind them was familiar.

"Dr. Thomas."  Yvonne turned to greet him.  "Thank you for agreeing to talk to us."

"You obviously like my company." He had one hand deep in the pocket of his long, black coat,  the other was holding his university scarf. His smile appeared forced.

Yvonne kicked off.  "We'd like to pick your brains, Dr. Thomas."

"Rhys, please..."

"Rhys, the last time we met, you told us about Llewelyn Ap Gruffudd's death by decapitation."

"It's not known, for sure, if he did die by decapitation. He may have had his head cut off after death."

"I see. Either way, we're interested to know what *you* think happened to his head. You said it wasn't interred with the rest of the remains."

"Is that what you asked me out here for? To find out where I think Llewelyn Ap Gruffudd's head is at?" He laughed out loud, putting his hand up to his forehead in a mocking gesture. "If I knew that, I'd probably be a *very* popular man with the historical society."

Yvonne frowned. "What *do* you think happened to his head, after it was cut off. What was its fate in the hours, days or weeks after his death."

"Sorry, Inspector, I shouldn't poke fun." Rhys ran his hand through his hair. "There are a few stories. I think it's pretty certain that it was sent to the English king, Edward, at Rhuddlan. It was reputedly shown off to the English soldiers stationed on Anglesey. It's said that Edward then had it sent on to London, where it was topped with a crown of ivy and displayed in the London pillory for a day. It was then carried atop a horseman's lance and placed on the Traitor's Gate at the Tower of London. It remained on display there for fifteen years."

The DI and psychologist's eyes met. Displayed on the gate of the Tower of London.

"He stayed here you know, at the Abbey, the night before he was killed. He and seven thousand of his men. He went to a meeting with his counsellors and was betrayed by his own countrymen."

"I can see the passion you feel for the story, Rhys." Tasha's expression was neutral, but the DI knew she was testing.

Rhys raised an eyebrow. "It's been my passion for the last decade."

**NINETEEN**

Yvonne tapped DCI Llewelyn's door and almost fell over as he opened it at the same moment she pushed against it.

With an embarrassed smile, she straightened herself. "sir, can I have a quick word?"

"Err... Can it wait? I'm about to meet with the Superintendent."

The DI looked like she might burst "Please?".

"All right, what is it? I can see that you'll explode if you don't tell me." He laughed, indulgently. "What have you been up to now?"

She gave him a don't-you-dare-patronise-me hard stare. "I think we'll need the help of London police."

"What for? We're in Wales..."

"I think David Davies' head may have been taken there."

"What?"

"I believe these murders are copies of historic or legendary deaths. I think our killer murdered Reverend Davies and then decapitated him, because Llewelyn, the last Prince of Wales, was killed and then decapitated."

"Where's this leading?"

"The prince's head was taken to London, and I feel sure that's where we'll find our victim's head."

"You're going to have to let me get my head around this. What you're suggesting is a bit of a stretch."

"Well, I was going to run it by you the other day, Chris, but it didn't seem like a good time."

"Very well. I'm seeing the Super in a minute. We're meeting with BBC representatives to discuss the details of this case for 'Crimewatch'. I was looking for you earlier, but I couldn't find you. I'll make sure we don't finalise anything until you and I have had a chance to discuss this, properly."

"Sir, I want to contact the Metropolitan and City Police forces, now, if that's all right with you. I think the head may have been taken to or near the Tower of London. Of course, it's just possible it could be anywhere in the city, but I strongly suspect that the tower is the most likely place. I've spoken to Dewi and he'll do the phoning round, if you're happy for us to go ahead."

"Do what you have to, but keep me informed, and I *mean* informed.

Yvonne was on her way back to Dewi, when he came hurtling along the corridor, out of breath, to find her. "Ma'am, you're not going to believe this..."

"What?" Yvonne stepped backward instinctively.

"It's all over the news, they've found a head in London!" Dewi spurted the words between rasping breaths.

"Male?"

"Yes, it's male. They're taking dental casts so that they can identify the victim."

"Seriously?"

"Do I usually run that hard up the stairs?" Dewi bent over, catching his breath.

"Err...no."

"The head was barely decomposed."

"Oh, our victim was killed weeks ago. There would definitely be substantial decomposition by now, unless it's been kept in cold storage. Perhaps it's not our victim."

"We'll fax over the dental records for Reverend Davies. If they match, it saves a family member the trauma of identification."

"Good, Dewi. Ask City police if there was any indication the head had been frozen or in cold storage."

"Will do."

"Oh, and Dewi?"

"Ma'am?"

"If it's confirmed, hunt down David Davies' family and inform them. I want them to hear it from us, not the newspapers."

"Righty-oh."

## TWENTY

Yvonne found Tasha in her temporary office.    "Have you heard?"

"I heard a commotion, what's happened?"

Yvonne brought her up to date.

"No way... So, in theory, if any of our suspects have been to London in the last week,  they're squarely in the frame."

"If it's David Davies' head, then a whole bunch of new angles open up.  We may get CCTV."

"By the way, I don't think Rhys Thomas is our murderer."

"I thought you might say that, I saw the look on your face when we left the abbey."

"If he were our murderer, he wouldn't have been able to stop himself looking at the place he left the body.  Our killer was very careful forensically, but that doesn't mean that he wouldn't go through self-doubt. He'd have been subconsciously checking that he hadn't missed anything or left anything behind..."

"And?"

"I didn't see him look, once."

"So, not our killer."

"If he's our killer, he controlled his natural impulses very well."

Yvonne worked in the incident room into the evening, moving photographs and pieces of information around on the board, drawing and re-drawing lines and connections. She didn't realise how tired she'd become.

A confident knock on her office door forced her to pause.

"Come in."

DCI Llewelyn poked his head around her door. "I thought I might go to the Chinese for some food. Fancy it?"

Yvonne leaned back and ran both her hands through her hair. "Take out, you mean?"

"Or sit in, I'm easy..."

If she'd been more awake, Yvonne would have raised an eyebrow. As it was, she rubbed both her eyes and nodded. "I *am* hungry. In fact I've just realised that I am famished.

"Right, grab your coat and we'll get something."

As they left the station for their respective cars, it was dark already, and he helped her on with her coat. "I have a spare room at my place, if you're too tired to drive home, after we've eaten." He looked awkward and Yvonne wondered, for the first time, whether he might actually fancy her.

"That's a kind offer, Chris, but I need to get home."

He looked down at the ground, cleared his throat and rubbed his head. She felt guilty and nearly told him that it wasn't that she didn't want to stay at his, just that she preferred her own bed. *Especially*, when she was as tired as she was now. The words stayed in her head, however, and the moment passed.

They parked their cars just outside 'The Lotus' Chinese restaurant, just off Broad Street. The DCI waited as she stepped out of the car. "Are you sure this is okay?" he asked, with genuine concern. "I'll understand if you're too tired."

She smiled and touched his arm. "I'm starving. Come on. Let's eat."

They were shown to a table near a giant cheese plant, around to the bottom-left of the L-shaped room. Only two of the other tables were occupied. Yvonne was glad. The soft, background music and the intoxicating smell of the food being prepared were what she needed, after her long day. She closed her eyes and breathed. The muscles in her back relaxed and her shoulders dropped. When she opened her eyes again, the DCI was watching her. His eyes flicked to the menu in his hands.

"This was a good idea," Yvonne said, to break the awkwardness. "It smells great. I hadn't realised how hungry I was. I'd lost track of the time."

"I know." Chris Llewelyn nodded. "This case has been getting to everyone. How have you been getting on with your psych sessions?"

"You mean my torture sessions..." Yvonne scowled.

"I *mean* your psych sessions," the DCI laughed.

"They're just about endurable. Problem is, every time I go into Dr. Rainer's room, I feel like a petulant child going into teacher's office. I can't seem to help myself. I can't believe that woman's patience."

"I think, sometimes, you are your own worst enemy. You go about searching for the next stick to beat yourself."

Yvonne sighed. "Perhaps you're right, but it's not so much that I want to beat myself, more that I'll do pretty much anything to chase down a murderer."

"Including putting yourself in danger..."

Yvonne switched her gaze to the reflections in the window. "Tell me about the Crimewatch programme, when will you be appearing on it?"

"It's all happening the day after tomorrow. We'll be live from nine o'clock. I think our appeal is first up. We should have the ID of the head found in London by then, and know whether or not it's our victim. I got your report this morning, that will be a great help. I'll run through it with you some time tomorrow."

"No problem, I just hope we get a name for the perp – a concrete person to investigate. There are so many elements to these crimes, it's a very confusing picture." Yvonne leaned to one side, to allow the waiter to place their meals. "This killer is going to great lengths to muddy the waters."

The DCI listened, as she poured her heart out about the case. As she fell asleep that night, she mused that he was a very good listener. He should have been her psychiatrist.

The following morning, CID was awash with activity: phone calls to and from City of London police; preparations for the appearance on Crimewatch; and more information being added to the story board, with Yvonne and Dewi trying to piece it all together.

They'd received confirmation the head was that of Reverend Davies. Yvonne had wanted to call the relatives, but the DCI insisted that he take on that responsibility.

Tasha joined Yvonne and Dewi as they added the photographs, taken by City of London SOCO, to the board.

"So, now we have it confirmed he's basing his kills on historical events." Tasha pursed her lips as she examined the London Photographs. "The first picture shows the head where it was found, on the spike of a metal railing close to the Tower of London. The other photos show the various stages of the forensic investigations and the dental moulds. Macabre, aren't they?"

"Yes." Yvonne stood back from the board, hands on hips. "Even more macabre is the fact the killer kept the head in his freezer for several weeks."

"Imagine looking at it every time you went to get some frozen chips..." Dewi pulled a face.

"Yes, okay, Dewi, we get the picture..." Yvonne gave him a mock disapproving look.

162

"He's certainly a cool customer, I'll give him that." Tasha tapped her pen on her hand. But why wait? Why wait several weeks before taking the head to London? What caused the delay?"

"Maybe it was too hot for him to take it straight there?" Dewi scratched his head.

"Or, maybe he was busy doing something else and couldn't get the time to go to London until weeks after the killing. If so, why? What was he doing?" Yvonne sat on a chair, still studying the board.

"Well, we know one thing he was up to in that time..." Tasha also took a seat.

"We do?" Yvonne raised her eyebrows.

"Terrorising and killing Meirwen Ellis."

"Of course." Yvonne's eyes widened. "That was a big difference with Meirwen. The killer left his calling card *before* he murdered her. That didn't happen with any of the other victims."

"But, we had protection on Meirwen..."

"Yes. We did, but not the day he left the calling card. He could have killed her then, but he didn't. Why?"

"Maybe he was having second thoughts?" Dewi drank from his mug.

"Perhaps something in her demeanour made him postpone. Maybe he was wrestling with himself over whether to go through with it. Maybe he liked her." Yvonne was thinking again of Peter Griffiths.

"He took her to Capel Celyn, what was the relevance of that?" Tasha walked up to the board. "Yes, people were displaced and yes, a whole village was flooded with water, but no one died there – not for the benefit of the reservoir, anyway."

"I agree, that bit doesn't make sense at the moment, but there must be some meaning to her being taken and killed in that place." Yvonne sighed and got to her feet. "Let's get a coffee. I've got to brief the DCI in five."

He shifted from foot to foot and cleared his throat several times. His first couple of sentences were stilted and there was an uncharacteristic stutter. She'd been there herself and felt the fear: Crimewatch was a big deal. Yvonne recalled her time on it with absolute clarity: the appeal to find the Shotover Sadist. Now, she witnessed Chris Llewelyn going through the same nerves in the hunt to find the killer the press had dubbed, 'The Priest Slayer.' She was very glad that it wasn't she who was sweating the cameras.

They were glued to the TV: Yvonne, Dewi, Tasha, and several other officers from CID. All had descended on Yvonne's house for the 9 pm show. They watched as the DCI calmly outlined the events and described the effects on the family and friends of the deceased. He appealed for the public to piece together the characteristics attributed to the killer, in Tasha's profile.

He had done them proud, and the team cheered loudly in Yvonne's lounge as the presenters thanked DCI Llewelyn for his contribution, and moved on to the next appeal.

"And now we wait..." Dewi perched on the end of the sofa.

Yvonne sat back, next to him. "Now we wait..."


Bishop Dafydd Lewis beckoned her into the community centre, in the village of Bettws. He'd just finished giving a speech, about the changes planned for the church in Wales. Yvonne had wanted to be there for the whole talk, but had been delayed by various things. No matter, he had agreed to an interview, and that was far more important.

He looked relaxed, and more casually dressed than she'd expected, wearing jeans and a shirt.

"Thank you for agreeing to see me," she began.

"You're welcome, Inspector, I'm only too pleased to help, if it aids in the catching of this killer. So, what can I do?"

"Bishop, can you outline to me the changes which are taking place in the church in Wales?"

"There's lots going on, how much time have you got?"

Yvonne cleared her throat, pen at the ready. "As much time as you need. I believe our killer's motivation is rooted in his resistance to change."

The bishop raised his eyebrows. "Really? I see...Well, back in July we had a major report released, from three prominent Anglicans, advocating wide-ranging changes in the church. There were lots of reasons for this: low morale within the clergy; low congregation numbers; and too many church buildings, apparently, due to the reduced number of clergy and worshippers. Not enough funds to justify keeping them open."

"And this was back in July..."

"Yes."

"That was after our murders started."

"Yes, but the review was commissioned in July 2011. The contents of the report were no real surprise: leaks had been happening almost from the start."

"I see. Sorry, please go on."

"The Archbishop of Wales knew the church had problems and agreed that changes were needed. The church in Wales will be celebrating its centenary in 2020. The report was commissioned to aid restructure, and reinvention of the church, by that date. Get it fit for the future, so to speak."

"To help it survive?"

"Quite."

"Go on..."

"There were around fifty recommendations in the report. They included things like training lay people to play a bigger role in church leadership; holding sermons on days other than the traditional Sunday; replacing parishes with so-called super-parishes: amalgamations of about twenty-five smaller parishes. Also, so-called ministry areas; giving some churches over for use by the whole community, and selling off others. They suggested working more closely with other denominations and prioritising the increased use of Welsh in sermons."

"How were these recommendations decided?" Yvonne's pen was running out. She reached into her handbag and produced another one, scribbling madly, until the ink began to flow.

"They canvassed over a thousand people who attended open meetings. It was decided the church was simply not doing enough to reach out to the young."

"Any thoughts on why the church has declined so much?"

"Technology, possibly, or maybe the need for an excuse to be able to do what one likes instead of conform to religious order?" There was a sudden harshness in his voice. "Some Assembly members believe it's because the Archbishop is too political."

"Is that what *you* think?"

He straightened his back. "Inspector, religion has always walked side-by-side with politics. After all, the ten commandments were the first real laws, weren't they?"

Yvonne thought that unlikely, but refrained from saying so. "Have a lot of churches closed?"

He looked at her as though she were a small child. "A chapel closes, on average, every week, Inspector."

"Wow."

"Wow, indeed. The problem is not just confined to Wales, although I think it is felt especially keenly here. Christianity in Europe has been failing to adapt to an increasingly sceptical, and secular, population."

"Bishop Lewis, I have to ask you, do you suspect the involvement of any of your clergy in these devastating murders?"

"No. And, forgive me for asking, why would you single out my diocese? There have been murders in two others besides mine. Granted, the killings started here, but...really..."

Yvonne sat up straight. "Peter Griffiths appears very vocal in his resistance to change."

"Peter? Yes, but he's a good vicar. Being involved in the debate, does not a killer make. In any case, he was one of a group of clergy who voted *for* allowing female bishops."

"There are religious overtones to these killings, and the killer had access to paperwork for the rite of consecration."

"That sort of information is freely available on the web, Inspector. Any psychopath can make a murder appear connected to religion, if he wants to. I can't think of one good reason why a member of my clergy would be involved."

Yvonne had upset him, and that hadn't been her intention. "I'm sorry if I've offended you."

Bishop Lewis sighed deeply. "Go on with your questions, Inspector."

"How much contact do clergy from the various diocese have with each other?"

"Quite a lot, really. It's normal for them to meet up, discuss ecclesiastical matters, form friendships, and go out together. That's truer of the ordinary clergy, than it is of someone like myself. I don't know, so well, the clergy from other diocese. Why do you ask that, anyway?" His eyes had narrowed.

"Reverend Peter Griffiths was good friends with Meirwen Ellis, from the diocese of Swansea and Brecon."

"Yes, I understand she shared some of his feelings, regarding the decline of the church in Wales."

"What's *your* feeling about all the changes?"

"You can't stop progress, Inspector, and besides, I'm retiring in a few years."

"What will happen then?"

"Now that, is top secret."

"Top secret?"

He pursed his lips. "We have a peculiar system for selecting a new bishop here in Wales. It makes me think of the Vatican and the choosing of the pope." He smiled, as he waited for her reaction.

"Sorry, I don't know anything about the choosing of the pope, you'll have to elaborate."

"Basically, it's a secret sort of process. Carried out behind closed doors, over three days, by something called an electoral college."

"An electoral college?" Yvonne was still making copious notes.

"An electoral college is a collection of forty-seven members, which includes at least three clergy and and a few lay people. The members themselves have to be voted for, every three years. They use a secret process to decide on their choice of bishop. If they fail to reach a decision, the bench of bishops take over and make the decision for them."

"And the bench of bishops are?"

"The collective bishops from all the diocese of Wales."

"I see... So that will happen when you retire."

"Yes, it will."

"Who gets the opportunity to be put forward for the position of bishop?"

"Pretty much any of the clergy, with experience, can try. Since 2012, that includes women."

"That was a difficult change for the church, wasn't it?"

"It was made possible by the extra votes of the Lay members of the church."

"I'd heard it was a close-run thing." Yvonne eyes didn't leave the bishop's face. "In England, they voted against in 2012, didn't they?"

His eyes narrowed. "The Church in Wales voted against it in 2008."

"But changed their minds..."

"After the massive controversy the vote against created, they looked at it again, and the decision was reversed." He stretched his back once more and looked bored with the interview. Yvonne felt she had all she needed for now, in any event.

"Right, well, Bishop Lewis, thank you for your time. If you think of anything else which you think relevant, please contact me," she said, rising from her seat.

"I will, Inspector."


"Boy, that was tough." Yvonne threw her bag down on a table in the CID tea-room .

Tasha was seated on top of a desk, having a break. "What's up?"

"I've just interviewed the bishop of St. Asaph again, and he's unwilling to even consider that a member of his clergy could be involved in the killing of other priests."

"Well, put yourself in his shoes. If someone came in here, asking you if you thought  one of your officers might be involved in a bunch of serial killings, what would you say?  What would you want to believe?  Imagine it...Dewi? Me? The DCI?"

Yvonne screwed her face up.  "That's different."

"Different how?"

Yvonne had got it already, but resisted for the hell of it.   "We're police officers. We *solve* murders."

"And they're clergy, *they* do good at all times."

Yvonne pushed out her tongue.  Tasha giggled.

The chilly, moonless, October night hung littered with stars. The Milky Way, clearly visible for the first time this year, gave a spectacular backdrop, as his breath made faint puffs of steam.   He fastened his wax jacket and crossed the yard to the barn, taking long strides, his shotgun tucked under his armpit.

The barn door wobbled, one of the hinges barely attached. He'd been meaning to fix it but just hadn't gotten around to it.  If he didn't do it soon, the door would fall off. He climbed the lopsided ladder to the old hay loft, each step softly complaining.

At the top, he moved a couple of hay bales, and wiped away the loose straw with his hand. The small hatch opened with a creak and he peered inside, using a torch he pulled from his pocket, and breathed a sigh of relief. The rolled up black cloth was still there, folded as he had left it.   He put his hand in to check the firmness. Yes, definitely undisturbed.

He checked it most nights. He had to. There were times he couldn't sleep if he didn't.  If they located Griff's gun, they located him. He should get rid of it, but he kept it - just in case.

He took out the roll of material, freed the gun parts, and started polishing them. They didn't need polishing, but this was part of his ritual. It gave him reassurance.

When he'd finished, he placed the parts neatly back in the cloth, in the correct order, and placed the whole thing back into the hatch. He stared at it, for several seconds, memorising how it looked, so he'd know if anyone touched it. Then, closing the hatch, he trod softly down the rickety wooden ladder and into the night.

## TWENTY-ONE

"My God, that's a lot of boxes." Dewi sighed, loosening his tie and pushing one of the offending boxes with the tip of his pen, a look of dread on his well-lined face.

The DI was busy cross-checking names on her tick list and organising the boxes according to date. "It is, Dewi, but these boxes may contain our killer."

"Bit *small,* isn't he?"

"Ha ha. What we have here are application forms, completed by most of the clergy in Wales, from when they were fresh out of university, or changing jobs."

"What are we looking for?"

"Would you be pissed at me if I said I'll know when I find it?"

"Yes."

"Well, it's a mixture of things, really: life experience, interests – a coming together of certain elements of the candidate's life journey."

"Nice and easy then..."

"Think,  an avid interest in history, political affiliations, protest groups, university societies – that sort of thing."

"Best get stuck in then."

"I'll make a start, Dewi, if you get the coffee."

"Right you are, ma'am."

Supping steaming hot coffees, they commenced sorting out those clergy relevant to local parishes.

"We go through the victims' files, too."

"Right you are."

"If you come across Peter Griffiths before I do, give me a shout."

"How long we going to spend on this, ma'am?"

"As long as it takes, Dewi. As long as it takes."

They hadn't even completed the first two boxes, when they were disturbed by raised voices in the corridor. Yvonne rose from her seat and opened the door to see Tasha storming down the corridor and an irritated DCI Llewelyn glowering after her.

"What's up?" Yvonne asked Tasha, as she brushed past.

"Ask *him!*" Tasha didn't slow her pace and disappeared through the door at the end of the corridor.

"What was all that about?" Yvonne turned her attention to the DCI.

"Don't ask..."

Yvonne stood, open-mouthed, as the DCI strode back into his office, the door rebounding with a loud bang.

Yvonne walked back to Dewi, shrugging her shoulders, the look of surprise still on her face.

"Just another day at the office, ma'am," Dewi laughed, unconcerned.

"I hope Tasha's all right, the DCI can be an ass, at times." Yvonne blew her breath out between pursed lips, as she returned to her seat.

"They'll be right as rain, later." Dewi looked around at the boxes. "Last thing we need is distractions if we're gonna get through this little lot."

"You're right. No more distractions."


Yvonne had Meirwen Ellis' résumé in her hands. She paused before opening it, a wave of sadness engulfing her. It felt like prying, but that was her job, and Meirwen's family deserved closure. Feeling that she'd already let the reverend down once, she had no intention of doing so again.

Most of the contents came as no real surprise. Meirwen had begun studying Divinity in 1992, not that long after women were first allowed to join the clergy. She noted her hobbies as swimming, reading and socialising – all normal for a young woman.

As the DI flicked through more of the file, a loose leaf of A4 paper fell to the floor. It was a letter, seemingly written by Meirwen herself, expressing an interest in a female bishop position, should one become available. The letter was dated January 2008.

"She had ambitions to become bishop, Dewi."

"Who did?"

"Meirwen Ellis. It looks like she expressed an interest *prior* to the vote in 2011."

"Can I have a look?" Dewi took hold of the letter.

"It's addressed to Bishop Dafydd Lewis."

"Anything else in the file?"

"No, nothing. Nothing that really stands out. How are you getting along?" Yvonne asked, eyeing Dewi's box.

"Just been through David Evans' file and nothing of note in there, either. No interests in history or nationalism. Looks like he supported females becoming bishops, from the notes."

"Well, I've got Peter Griffiths' file now. Let's see what we've got in here. I hope I haven't got us going through all this for naught."

"I doubt it'll be for naught, ma'am. If nothing else, we'll have a bit better understanding of our victims and potential perps."

"Hang on a minute..."

"Ma'am?"

"I've seen this symbol somewhere before."

"What symbol?"

"Looks like two sickles, crossed, with a spear in the centre."

Dewi rose from his seat again, to peer over her shoulder. "That's the 'Eryr Wen'. The White Eagle. The symbol of the Free Wales Army."

"It's been doodled on the bottom of a leave request form, in Peter Griffiths' file."

"Bingo. When was it done?"

"1995."

"A while back, then."

"There's something else...looks like he began his university career studying Welsh history.  He obtained a lower second class honours at Cardiff University, before going on to study theology, at St. Andrews."

"Are you thinking what I'm thinking?"

"This is enough to arrest him on suspicion, and interview him under caution.  Bingo!"

Tasha's car screeched and swerved, the psychologist swearing under her breath.   She was furious with the DCI.  Her heart racing, she still had a scowl on her usually placid face.  The DCI had calmly informed her that, due to budget constraints, he was dropping her from the case.  Her profile had been helpful, but she was no longer needed.

The psychologist wondered if the DI had been party to the decision?  She felt betrayed.  She'd been so sure that Yvonne needed her, having more to offer than just a one-stop profile.

Having stopped at the petrol station on New Road to fill up, she grabbed a cold orange juice from the fridge and decided to carry on driving.  She programmed her sat nav for LLyn Celyn.  Still having a need to figure out the killer, she decided to go to the place where he'd taken the life of Meirwen Ellis.

An hour and a half later, she  pulled up beside Llyn Celyn resevoir, stepping out onto it's stony bank.  The water had receded greatly, exposing tree stumps like giant, gnarled spiders or disembodied hands.  She imagined they might crawl, at any moment, along the mud.

She recalled the 'Cofiwch Dreweryn' she'd seen painted, on an old wall, on the road to Aberystwyth.  She'd found it on Google.  It meant 'remember Treweryn',  and had been written by those angry at the flooding of the tiny village.

The place *felt* sad.  She imagined the church bell tower, exposed in summer drought, ringing out as in the legend.

The sound of wheels on gravel caught her attention, and she peered along the bank.  Some distance away, the occupant got out and removed a bag from the boot, sitting at the water's edge to eat.  Why hadn't she thought of that?  She sat  on a bench, and stared out over the reservoir.  It was hard to feel angry in a place like this.  Her thoughts returned to the murderer.

What had Meirwen been thinking when she was brought here?  Did she know her killer?  Why had her killer brought her to this spot?  And what was the significance for him?

Her drowning surely alluded to the drowning of the village, but why?  What was all that about?  Why was this case proving so difficult to crack?

She leaned her arms on her knees, her chin on her hands, staring for several minutes and breathing deeply of the fresh, earthy air. More relaxed, she decided to return to Newtown later, to discuss the DCI's plan with Yvonne. She walked on, to the memorial for the drowned village of Capel Celyn. Not really sure what she expected, it definitely wasn't what she found.

A more understated memorial, she couldn't imagine. It had the appearance of being unfinished, and was more stark than she'd expected. Perhaps that had been the intention of its creator- a ruinous folly, a poor recompense for the picturesque village, drowned by the dam, for the benefit of industrial Liverpool.

It was little more than a series of walls, one of which was rounded to form a small room, with a glass-panelled front. A small cross adorned the top.

She tried the door. Locked. Peering through the glass, she could see a lectern with the names of the displaced, and could understand the strong feeling the drowning had created. But why murder? And why now?

At the time, activists had tried blowing up the dam, but never had they attempted murder. No, Tasha decided, this was not about the drowning of Capel Celyn. This had more to do with the killer losing control over his life, and equating it to these events.

Finally, she came to the small square graveyard. The headstones were arranged around the edges, as this was not the real graveyard of Capel Celyn, but rather the place where a few exhumed bodies had been reburied. The families just not able to bear their loved ones being under the soil, below that vast lake. Tasha had watched the eerie Youtube video footage of the ruins at the bottom.

She closed her eyes and sighed, it was time to leave. As she turned to go, something hard connected with the back of her head.

## TWENTY-TWO

Yvonne and Dewi were taking a well-earned break from their box-trawling.  Yvonne chased the DCI down the corridor, as he was about to leave the building.

"So, are you going to tell me why you were arguing with Tasha?" She tried to sound casual.

"I explained to her that we no longer require her services, now that we have the profile."

"What?"

"Well...we don't."

"You mean you don't think we can afford her."

"That, too."

"I need her help on this case."

"You don't need her help anymore."

"I do."

"You're using her as a crutch."

Yvonne glared at him, her colour heightening.    "Money shouldn't come into this."

He sighed heavily.   "Well, I'm afraid it does."

"I hope you told her I wasn't involved in your decision."

"The subject didn't come up."

"You should have consulted me, I'm the lead investigator."

"And I'm your superior officer, Yvonne."  He stretched to his full height.   "I'm paid to make these decisions.  I have to go..."

He turned on his heal, leaving the angry Yvonne boring holes in the back of his head.

"Are you okay, ma'am?" Dewi joined her , treading cautiously.

Yvonne was still glaring, "I have to make sure she stays."

Someone had played rubgy-football with her head. Tasha winced as she came round, due to a sore patch on the side of her head. She squinted in the dim light, making out her surroundings using the sliver of light emitted from a small strip of LEDs.

She found herself in a damp, stone structure, about eight foot by six, with her hands tied behind her back. The cord was only just shy of cutting her skin. Listening for any sign of her jailer, she could hear nothing save for the occasional drip, drip, coming from somewhere in the corner.

She rocked to her feet, wincing again at the stiffness in her legs. Placing an ear to the cold, dank stone, she listened for any sign of the outside. Hearing only the pumping of her own blood in her ears, she called out several times but got no response. In the end, she gave up – sitting down again, to get her head straight.

She worked at her jumper with her knees and  chin, until her knees were partially covered, and she could warm them against her belly. Then, placing her chin on them, she contemplated her situation.

The presence of a large stone casket, meant this had to be a tomb, or perhaps a mausoleum, but there was no indication of where it might be. She'd been unconscious, since being hit on the head, so had no idea of how long it had taken to get here.

A heavy door grated open and her jailer entered, shining a torch directly at her so she couldn't see his face. She blinked in the harsh light, lowering her eyes to ease the discomfort.

"This is not personal. I know why you're here. I know who you're working with. I do not hold that against you, but that won't stop me from killing you." The disembodied, robotic voice penetrated the silence. He was using text-to-speech.

"Do I know you? Have we met?" The fact he'd disguised his voice gave Tasha hope that he didn't intend killing her.

"The less you know, the better. Here's some food." The figure placed an open pack of sandwiches on the ground with an open bottle of water. From his outline, she suspected he was wearing a balaclava.

He left her trying to eat and drink, her hands still tied behind her back. She hadn't had the chance to ask him to loosen her bindings, to lessen the pain in her wrists. She realised that she must know who he was, or he wouldn't have bothered to disguise himself. Her brain ached from mulling over the identity of her captor, and she turned her attention to the food and drink, consuming it any way she could. Not knowing how long she would be there, or when her next meal might come, she ate everything.

Dewi drew the car to halt, just short of the old, Norman church, in Tregynon. The Sat Nav indicated this as the place, and Yvonne eyed the surroundings through the window, looking for the cottage of Peter Griffiths.

She found it easily, the aptly named 'Church Cottage', stood out and yet sat easy within its surroundings. It was clearly a Tudor building, being black and white and not a ninety degree angle anywhere.

"We're here, ma'am." Dewi slid out of his seat and stretched, as the DI got out of hers. Still holding onto the door, she wondered if the killings were targeted slaughter, rather than an attack on Christianity itself.

A tiny paddock adjoined the garden. Yvonne spotted a Palomino horse, wearing a muddied coat. The horse snorted at them, and something in its eyes made her pause, as it approached the fence. A sadness. They gazed at each other in unspoken conversation for several seconds, before the DI continued down the garden path.

Yvonne had imagined the reverend's garden to be one of loud, sculptured plants – form over colour. She couldn't have been more wrong. This was more a garden of borders and flowering shrubs. Whoever tended this garden took time and effort.

Dewi banged on the door twice, to no avail. The curtains were drawn, so they were unable to see inside. Yvonne nodded to Dewi, and he put his shoulder to the door. It opened easily, and the surprised DS landed on the floor, jumping up and brushing himself off, a disgruntled look on his face. A quick examination of the lock explained why: the door was on the latch.

"Reverend Griffiths? Reverend Griffiths?" Receiving no reply, the DI proceeded into the small entry hall.

The smell hit her first. The mustiness clawed at the back of her nose, like a sniff of freshly ground pepper, and she sneezed. On the wall opposite, next to the lounge door, a montage of photographs of the reverend and who Yvonne took to be the reverend's daughter, were on display. They were smiling together in several, she being dressed in show jumping jacket and jodhpurs. The DI recognised a younger version of the horse, from the paddock outside. They looked so happy together, he with the intense pride of a father, and the girl ecstatically holding a trophy aloft, or else looking down from her horse, a rosette displayed clearly on its neck.

The DI tried to reconcile the man she saw in these pictures – the soft, indulgent father - with the strident, angry campaigner. She had to admit that she hadn't previously considered him as a rounded whole, and started to doubt her suspicions. And yet were not all killers also family members?

Dewi came back from checking out the kitchen and shook his head. "I'll check upstairs."

Yvonne nodded her assent, and followed him up.

On opening the bedroom door, she recognised the smell of death and felt her knees buckle.

"Oh, dear God." Dewi paused in the doorway.

There, on the bed, lay the cold, bloodied body of the reverend. His taut facial muscles, open mouth and wide eyes, knotted Yvonne's gut, depriving her of her breath.

"Are you okay, ma'am?" Dewi held out his hand, but she stiffened, not wanting to appear weak.

"I'm fine." Her answer was a little too terse, but Dewi was already turning his attention to calling it in, and requesting an ambulance.


The reverend's throat had been cut and his torso bared, in the familiar way of the priest slayer. Congealed blood would be washed away to revel the killer's message, and Yvonne knew all-too-well what that would be.

Her thoughts turned to the agitated horse and the loving daughter who, at this precise moment, had no inkling of the life-shattering news she was about to receive. Had the horse understood what had happened to his master, or had it been expecting a meal which never came? Yvonne was overcome with sadness as she left the cottage to await SOCO. She'd been way off. Instead of suspecting him, she should have offered him protection.

Once SOCO arrived, she grabbed the necessary coveralls, in order to take a proper look at the scene.

**TWENTY-THREE**

Reverend Griffiths' home was vastly different to the one they had entered, not an hour earlier. Yvonne, suited up and determined, cast a critical eye over the scene, now properly lit by daylight from the window and powerful SOCO lamps.

The reverend hadn't been a hoarder. In fact, quite the opposite. Perhaps, thirty years ago, someone had installed a fitted kitchen, but the doors on many of the cupboards were lopsided or, in one case, missing altogether. There wasn't a lot of food in the cupboards, and only enough crockery for two people. Even that was mismatched. The majority of the reverend's possessions appeared to be connected either to his daughter or the church, making it hard for Yvonne to get a full picture of the man the reverend had been.

It was only later, when she talked to his neighbours, opposite, that she learned that he liked to play piano. That he had possessed one once, but had donated it to a local school, when they were no longer able to tune theirs. Similarly, he regularly passed on food and clothes to the Red Cross and food banks. He was a man who had kept his doors open to others, whether from his parish or not, and he had often, wistfully, talked about his daughter whom, it would appear, no longer visited him much, and had two rapidly growing children of her own. The horse had grown old, but the reverend had not been able to bring himself to part with it.

All of this left Yvonne confused, to say the least, her main suspect not only the latest victim, but a thoroughly decent human being. What would Tasha make of this? Yvonne's thoughts turned to the psychologist, realising she still hadn't heard from her. She resolved to call the London Met, when she got back to the station.

It had arrived in a plain, brown envelope, with a printed label. An SD card, the Exif data of which had clearly been altered to disguise the sender and his equipment. This was the reason Yvonne had received ten missed phone calls on her mobile, whilst she'd no signal, in Tregynon. As she entered the station, all of CID were huddled around one computer in the main office.

They watched in stunned silence, a look of disbelief on all their faces. On the screen in front of them was a dark, grainy image of Tasha, her hands bound behind her back. She looked tired and in pain. The team could see nothing which identified where she was and there was no sound, except for a computer-generated voice-over informing them that she was being held captive until the time was right, in a few days, to drown her.

It wasn't shock which Yvonne felt, but something else. She had feared that this was the reason the psychologist hadn't been in touch. The DI knew that her friend, angry and upset she could no longer work the case, wouldn't take that lying down. Of course, she'd gone off on her own. Gone back to one of the crime scenes to get closer to the killer. And she'd gotten her wish and ended up very close. Too close. Way too close.

How could Tasha have been so reckless with her own safety, knowing what this killer was capable of? He'd had said he intended to drown the psychologist in a few days, meaning when? Assuming the video was fresh, that still gave them little time. The truth was, they had no idea exactly *when* the video was filmed, due to adulteration of the Exif data.

Dewi put a hand on her shoulder. "You okay?"

"Yes...No. What the hell did she think she was doing?"

"You think she went looking for him..."

"I think she went back to one of the crime scenes. Probably in a state, after her argument with Llewelyn."

"The team are waiting for a briefing, ma'am."

"I know, I want words with Llewelyn, first."

"Take it easy, ma'am." Dewi's expression was unusually firm and she knew he was right. If they were to find Tasha in time, it would require them all pulling together and reading from the same page. Didn't stop her feeling angry, though.

The door swung open and paper fluttered to the floor. The DCI ran a hand through his hair. "Which PC?"

"That one, sir." Yvonne pointed roughly in its direction. "It's a copy of the SD card. The original is with forensics."

"You think this is my fault." It was a statement more than a question.

"Do *you* think it's your fault?" Yvonne wasn't about to assuage his guilt.

"I didn't make her go after him."

"I don't believe she did go after him. I think she was following in his footsteps. In any event, sir, we've got a team to brief and we're already running out of time to find her."

"Point taken." Christopher Llewelyn strode to the front of the room, stilling the voices and refocusing minds.

He was giving instruction, but Yvonne, though listening, was also recalling parts of the video again. They didn't have a date on the SD card, at least not yet. Maybe the forensic bods could come up with some magic, she'd certainly seen that before. What they did have, however, was the postage date: yesterday. Now, supposing the video was filmed yesterday, the killer had said a few days, she hoped that meant they had at least a couple more days. On the face of it, the situation might seem hopeless, but the DI wasn't going to go there in her head. She was totally focused on the time she hoped they still had.

The DCI gave the floor to Yvonne.

"Okay, I want each of you to go to one of the crime scenes. Don't go alone. Take at least two uniformed officers. If you see Tasha's vehicle, or any other sign she may have been where you are, I want you to call myself or the DCI, immediately. Call for back up and leave the scene intact for SOCO and the search teams." Yvonne paused and drew in a deep breath. "The killer told us he intends to drown Tasha in the next few days. We know that he chooses sites of historical significance. Myself and DS Hughes will be working on finding out which body of water he intends to use. Be vigilant at all times. This killer is a real threat to all of us."

The DI's breakfast hit the back of the toilet bowl, spattering in all directions, as she held on to the toilet roll holder. Her head swam, her chest heaved, and she thought she might pass out. Afterwards, she felt relieved that she had held it together long enough to get the team out there. The one person who would have been invaluable in the task ahead was the very person whose life was in danger.

Twenty minutes later, and Dewi was pacing, waiting for her, obviously deep in thought.

"Dewi."

"Ma'am?"

"The historian, Rhys Thomas, gave you his phone number, didn't he?"

"He did, yes."

"Let's call him; find out where he is and what he's up to."

192

"Right you are."

Yvonne could hear clatter and tannoys in the background, along with the sound of airplane engines. "Rhys Thomas?" She raised her voice in response to the noise.

"Yes," he shouted back. "Listen, can I call you back? It's not convenient."

"Where are you?"

"Heathrow. Just flown back from a conference in the States."

"I'll call you back."

Yvonne gave two hard raps on the DCI's door.

"Come in."

He looked at her, and she could see that he was desperate to make amends, but wasn't sure how to go about it.

She felt sorry for him and sighed. "I need your help, sir."

"Of course...what can I do?" His surprise was evident from his raised eyebrows, as though he couldn't believe his luck.

"Rhys Thomas. I've just called him on his mobile. He stated he was at Heathrow. Said he just got back from a conference in America. From the din in the background, this could well be correct. But I'd like to verify it and, since the team are otherwise engaged, and you know him, I thought you might be able to help."

The DCI nodded. "I'll get on it right away. The Super is on his way to speak to me, apparently. This'll help delay the inevitable inquisition."

"Thank you, sir."

"Yvonne?"

"Sir?"

"Why do you want to know?"

"If he was in America, he didn't post the SD card. And if he didn't post the SD card, he's no longer on my list of suspects. And if he's no longer a suspect, he may be able to help us."

"The location of the water..."

"Yes."

"Right, Dewi, let's go." Yvonne tossed the car keys to her DS, who caught them deftly.

"Where we we off to, then?"

"Nantmel."

Dewi didn't ask why. He knew only too well how little time they had. He trusted his DI implicitly, and she had a determined look on her face. She was onto something.

They found Jim, the church verger, arranging flowers near the pulpit. He appeared thinner than Yvonne remembered, and his movements were slow.

Yvonne's footfall was soft, as she approached, but she cleared her throat to warn him him she was coming.

Jim turned quickly, his pose defensive.

"Sorry to disturb you, Jim," Yvonne began. "I wonder if we might have a word?"

Jim's face relaxed, somewhat, and he motioned them into the vestry. Meirwen's vestments still hung from the hook, on the back of the door.

Yvonne swallowed. "Jim, I'd like you to think back to the day when the bloodied collar was left behind the church."

Jim's forehead creased. "I remember it pretty well. It gave us a shock. It's hard to forget such a thing."

"I know." Yvonne looked briefly at her shoes, then back up to return the verger's gaze. "I asked the reverend if she'd seen anyone unusual that day. Anyone she hadn't been expecting, or that stood out to her, and she said not."

Jim nodded.

"Now, I'm asking if you remember seeing anyone who mightn't exactly have been expected, but for whom it might not have been unusual to make an appearance at the church."

"You mean in the congregation?" Jim put his finger to his forehead.

"Possibly, but most especially, clergy."

"Clergy..." Jim's forehead furrowed again and she knew he was seeing the congregation in front of him.

"If you like, we can go away for a bit, if it helps you think."

"Bishop Lewis." Jim clipped the words.

"The bishop?" Dewi took a step forward.

"Why would the bishop come to a small church service? I'd have thought he'd be too busy?"

"It's the sort of thing he does: drop in, occasionally, unannounced. Apparently, he does it for all the churches. I asked Meirwen, ages ago, why he did that, and she said he's a stickler for protocol and likes to know that things are being done correctly. She thought it was because he was afraid of people falling away from the church, from God. She thought him obsessive-compulsive."

"He suspects his own clergy of driving people way?" Dewi pulled a face.

"He's afraid of modern methods creeping in, putting off some of the older parishioners."

"Is he afraid of change?" Yvonne rubbed the scar on her chin.

"He was very vocal in the female bishop and gay clergy debates."

"I'm guessing anti-..."

"You guess right." Jim nodded emphatically and put a hand to the small of his back.

Yvonne understood it was time to leave, and looked sideways at Dewi, who blinked deliberately back.

"Thank you, Jim." Yvonne gave him a tender smile. "Might I light candle for the reverend?"

Jim smiled back, knowingly. "I'll get you one." It was almost a whisper.

Yvonne took the candle from from him and walked to the left side of the pulpit. A bunch of candles were already burning there. She bowed her head, a silent message to Meirwen, a promise to find her killer. Lighting the candle from those already alight, she set it down on a few drips of molten wax. She bowed her head, once more, and rejoined Dewi. They shook hands with Jim, and left.

On the way back, the DI was pensive.

"That puts the bishop right in the frame, doesn't it?" Dewi read her thoughts.

"Well, it certainly makes him more interesting. I'd like to know where he is and where he's been recently. I think we need to learn more about him, fast."

The DI's mobile bleated in her bag. She rooted around for it, cursing under her breath.

"DI Giles?"

"We've found Tasha's vehicle, ma'am. It's at Llyn Celyn."

"I knew it." Yvonne sucked air through her teeth. "Thank you for letting me know. Inform the DCI, if you haven't done so already, and get SOCO down there. Meanwhile, could you get a couple of cars down to Bishop Lewis' place and bring him in, please. Exercise caution, he could be armed and he may be dangerous. Ask the DCI to get an ARV on standby." Yvonne clicked the mobile off.

"Her car's at Llyn Celyn, Dewi. Let's get down there. She may still be in the locality."

Tasha's Audi appeared untouched and, they suspected, just as she'd left it. There were no keys in it. Yvonne peered through the window, as SOCO guys prepared it for towing away. There was a road map open on the passenger seat, a half consumed bottle of diet coke in the drinks holder, and an open packet of what looked like cheese and onion sandwiches. Yvonne stepped backwards and onto the foot of a photographer who yelped. What *was* it with photographers? She apologised, reluctantly.

"I don't think she expected to be long." Yvonne rejoined Dewi. "She was in the middle of lunch."

"They've had a good look around the water and the area surrounding. The search is ongoing, but it doesn't look like she's anywhere around here."

"No, he's taken her away, somewhere. If he was keeping her here, he'd have disposed of the car." Yvonne didn't really know why she'd come. They were rapidly running out of time. There was little she could add to what was already being done here, by SOCO and uniform. "You'll probably think me odd, Dewi." She gave a wry smile. "I just thought I might *sense* something."

Her phone rang again. This time, she had only to retrieve it from her coat pocket, "DI Giles..."

The officer on the other end sounded out of breath. "He's not here, ma'am."

"Who's not?"

"Bishop Lewis. We've talked to neighbours and they suggest a small-holding he sometimes visits, owned by his father, in Pembroke. Shall we head up there?"

"Yes, do that. Oh...and make sure you have plenty of back up."

"Will do, ma'am."

Yvonne looked tired, and drained. "We can't fail, Dewi. We just mustn't."


It took around forty minutes to get back to the station. DCI Llewelyn greeted them at the door.

"Yvonne." He handed her a note. "Dr. Rhys Thomas was in America. I verified it with the conference organisers. He gave a plenary lecture, yesterday morning, before getting his flight back. Well over two hundred people watched him deliver it."

"Thank you." Yvonne looked him straight in the eyes, and her look was softer than he'd seen it in days. "and I mean that."

He nodded gently in response.


Rhys Thomas sat in reception. The DI walked swiftly to collect him and take him through to an interview room.

"Don't worry about the room." She put a coffee down on the table for him. "I'm not going to interrogate you, but you may be able to help us."

"Go on." Rhys Thomas cocked his head and narrowed his eyes. "I'll help if I can."

"We'll need you to keep it to yourself. Someone's life is depending on it." She waited for that to register.

"Of course."

"Is there an important Welsh anniversary coming up in the next two to three days...today, tomorrow, the next day?"

His eyes narrowed again.

Yvonne continued, "It will be associated with water. A body of water. A large body of water in Wales."

She was struck by how vague and desperate this was sounding, and felt fear move up through her, a fine covering of sweat developing on her skin. "It may be related to Llyn Celyn. But it may not be." Talk about a shot in the dark.

Rhys loosened his tie and leaned back in his chair, puffing out his cheeks, which he let go with a loud puhh sound. "You'll have to give me some time."

"How long?"

"Couple hours, maybe? Tomorrow morning at the latest. I have some ideas but I'll need to check dates." He rose from his chair. "I'll let you know as soon as I can."

Yvonne looked directly into his eyes, her own earnest. "We'll be waiting for you."

It felt like the cold had eaten through every cell of her body. Tasha wanted to move. She knew if she didn't she may become incapable, yet, every part of her felt leaden. The pain in her wrists had numbed, but between her shoulder blades really ached, and shifting position didn't stop it.

There was a part of her that just wanted to give in to the cold and damp. To just let the deep sleep take over. And yet, she still had fight within her. Enough to keep telling herself that the DI would find her and this killer would be punished.

She'd been thinking about Yvonne, about everything they had been through. About how she had chastised the DI for being so foolish as to get caught by the 'Shotover Sadist'. Now, she had done a similarly foolish thing. She could just picture Yvonne's reaction, and was sorry for the panic and stress she knew this would have caused. They say that necessity is the mother of invention, and Tasha prayed that this was the case with the team. She hoped her situation would speed up, not slow down, the resolution of this case.


"Wake up. We have to get ready."

She struggled to open her eyes. How had she fallen asleep? She didn't want to wake up. Didn't want to respond.

"I said, wake up."

Speak and spell was back. Her older cousins had owned a 'Speak and Spell' when they were all very young. She had loved the way it reacted when her cousins deliberately spelled words wrong just to get it to tell them they were 'incorrect!" Funny how she thought of this now.

She could see his shape and the balaclava on his head. He placed the tablet down, but it continued talking, even as he placed a bag over her head and pulled her, roughly, to her feet. Her legs didn't want to prop her up. She had fallen against him and didn't even have the strength to barge into him, which was what she wanted to do.

Being a psychologist, she knew she ought to be working on becoming his friend, but didn't have the strength and, more to the point, the thought made her sick to the stomach.

He placed a sandwich in her mouth, and she *wanted* to eat, because she wanted to live, but was gagging uncontrollably, and he dropped it to the floor. She cried, then, for the first time. Loud sobs, which would have melted the hearts of most, but not his.

He continued to force her boots back onto her feet, then making her stand up. As she couldn't see, she hit the wall on the way out of her prison, and swore at the unexpectedness. He half-pulled, half-dragged her to a vehicle and shoved her in the boot. This was the warmest she had felt.

It took Yvonne and Dewi around two hours to drive down to Pembroke, where they joined those officers already on site. The bishop's family farm lay close to Tenby, on the Pembrokeshire coast.

The DCI was doing his face-of-the-investigation bit, and Yvonne resisted the urge to head off in another direction, when he approached.

"Bishop Lewis isn't here," he began. "His father is in the farmhouse, over there."

Yvonne took in the large group of buildings, and the land which appeared to roll into the sea. The views were quite something. Next to the quadrangle of buildings, the road ran through a little coppice of deciduous trees.

"It's a big farm," she said, finally. "Does the bishop's father still work it?"

"No, he says he doesn't any more. He has three sons, and the eldest, the bishop's half-brother, John, does most of the heft, helped out by another brother, Hugh."

"Did he say how often the bishop comes down here?"

"It's not a regular occurrence, apparently, just the occasional weekend. The frequency of visits dropped off a bit after his mother died, a couple of years ago. He was down here for two weeks, whilst on leave, recently."

"Are we able to look around?"

"As long as we leave things as we found them. I wouldn't like to get on the wrong side of the old man..."

Yvonne signalled to Dewi, motioning him in the direction of the barns.

"I reckon this farm has to be worth a few million."

Dewi creaked open the long, rusted-iron gate, leading them into the main courtyard. They were met with the smell of slurry, or silage, the DI was never quite sure which as they both smelled similar to her.

"Couple of hundred acres."

A strong Welsh accent delivered the last, and the DI turned to look at the elderly gentleman who had spoken. His ruddy face and his bronzed, leathery arms fitted with a man of the land. He looked as though he still had some strength in those wiry arms.

"Wow, that's impressive." She smiled. "I was admiring your view down to the sea."

"Swanlake Bay. There's a beach down there as well, thee'st know. I'm Ieuan Lewis."

"Nice to meet you, Mr. Lewis. Swanlake Bay, what a beautiful name. It suits it." She tucked a lock of stray hair back behind her ear. "What sort of farm do you run, Mr. Lewis?"

"Dairy. We did do a bit of B&B as well, at one time - when my wife was alive," he paused, as though seeing his wife's face in his mind's eye. "Anyway, we don't do much of that now. What are you looking for? And why are you looking for my son?"

"Mr. Lewis, you are *aware* that members of the clergy have been murdered?"

"Do you think my son is in danger?" She saw his body stiffen, as though the thought had not occurred to him.

"As far as we know, any member of the clergy could, potentially, become a victim." She'd decided to keep it simple. "We're looking for any signs that the killer may have been around here. We suspect he stalks his victims, for a time, prior to killing them." She felt guilt, at the sudden look of horror on his face. "But it's unlikely he's been here...we're just taking precautions."

The muscles in his face relaxed again and he took a step backwards, his signal for them to carry on. As they walked away, Yvonne tugged on Dewi's arm. "Go on ahead. Ask the guys to keep a lid on it, if they find anything. I don't want to frighten the father."

"Right you are, ma'am," Dewi nodded in agreement.

Yvonne passed the milking shed, and could see the stalls and metal piping, ready for the next shift. A middle-aged man in muddied, dark-blue overalls, was busy washing down the floor, his sleeves rolled up, displaying similarly tanned and muscled arms, though less leathery than his father.

"John?" She stepped forward into the shed.
He put down his brush, wiping his hands down the front of his overalls. "Hugh," he stated, with a strong Welsh lilt.

"I'm sorry, Hugh." The DI gave a self-deprecating smile. "I'm DI Giles, we're investigating a series of murders."

"What has that got to do with us?" There was no harshness in the question, yet it was delivered in a surprised, but interested, tone. He may be middle-aged, but there was an innocence in this man. She had sensed the same in the father, the innocence    of those who have led a certain, sheltered existence, that was rare in today's world.

"We wanted to check on your brother, the bishop." She bit her lip and scratched her head.

"Are you worried he may be next?"

"We need to keep an eye on everyone who could, potentially, become a victim."

"I see...Your colleagues are going through the barns.  What are they looking for?"

Yvonne liked the sing-songy way he delivered his words.  She was really coming to love her new home.  "Would you be disappointed if I said we won't know until we find it?"

He grinned at her.  "Are you looking for a needle?  There's a lotta hay in those barns."  He emphasised his joke with a wink.

She couldn't help but smile, and coloured at his flirtatious gesture.  She cleared her throat.  "I'll let you get on."


"Oh, aye?" Dewi gave her a knowing look. "Behave, ma'am, we've got work to do."

"Dewi, on your bike."   She pushed out her tongue. "Anything?"

"No. Nada. What now?"

"Well, we still haven't located the bishop, so that has to be our priority."   Her face became stern. "We're running out of time."

She felt her stomach sinking, that familiar feeling of despair and doubt.  She could see Tasha's face, could see that pleading look in her eyes, as she'd stared into the camera.  Yvonne had known that look was for her.  Dewi put a hand on the DI's elbow.

"Ma'am!"  DC Thomas came running towards them, his mobile phone still attached to his ear.

"Shhh, not so loud," she said as Dewi looked nervously towards the house.    "What is it?"

"They've found a gun in the top barn: a sighted-rifle, well hidden, but the dog found it."

"Okay, Thank you, DC Thomas."

Now, she faced a dilemma: did she go to the family and ask if they knew about the gun, potentially alerting the killer and Tasha's abductor? Or should they just take it? In the end, the decision was made for her. DCI Llewelyn ordered the gun be taken for ballistics, stating that, in his opinion, the whole family were now potential suspects and were, therefore, to be kept in the dark, until the bishop was located. Only then, he'd decided, could the whole family be taken in for questioning.

Yvonne didn't believe, for one moment, that the rest of the family were involved. The bishop had just become suspect number one.

**TWENTY-FOUR**


Dr. Rhys Thomas was pacing about reception, as Yvonne and Dewi walked into Aberystwyth station.  Yvonne had a voicemail on her mobile, saying he would meet her there.

As they approached, Dewi raised an eyebrow.  "I thought you didn't like him?"

"I changed my mind." Yvonne quickened her step into reception.  "What have you got?" she asked, immediately, there being no time for the luxury of niceties.

Rhys Thomas understood, he was also a busy man, and he recognised urgency when he saw it.  "Right, well, as you suggested, I used Capel Celyn as my starting point."

"Go on."  Yvonne guided the historian to an interview room, ignoring the dirty look she was given by the receptionist.

"Okay." Rhys Thomas looked excited by his involvement in the case, and  Yvonne wondered what Tasha might make of that.  "Treweryn was drowned because Liverpool was desperate for water.  It was drowned against the wishes of the Welsh people, and even the whole of the Welsh parliament - thirty-five of the thirty-six  MP's voted against it. But, and this is the important bit."  He licked his lips.  "It wasn't the first village to be drowned."

"Go on..." Yvonne leaned forward in her chair, across the small desk from Rhys, who continued, despite her penetrating stare unnerving him. "At the time Treweryn was flooded, there were very few pure-Welsh villages left in Wales. The language was already dying. It's why we hear so much about the drowning of that village - about the dam that is Capel Celyn. However..." It was Rhys' turn to lean forward in his chair, to stare at the detective. "Like I said, it wasn't the first village to be flooded in that way. Llanwddyn was."

"Llanwddyn. Where's that?" Yvonne could feel her gut shaking.

"The original Llanwddyn is underneath Lake Vernwy. The current village is a displaced version, built next to the lake. From Newtown, you take the road for Welshpool and Llanfair Caereinion. You go through Llydiart and it isn't that far from there...couple of miles. Anyway, at the time Llanwddyn was flooded, there were many Welsh-speaking villages. It wasn't such a big deal, so it isn't the first place you think of when you think of the English damming of Welsh waters. In fact, England has apologised for Treweryn, but not for Llanwddyn."

"And the date? What was the date for the drowning of Llanwddyn?"

"Well, that's where it gets more complicated." Rhys looked pained. "The valley was flooded over the period of about a year. The valves were closed, to allow the flooding, on 28th November, 1888."

"28th November...that's tomorrow."

"Yes." Rhys scraped his teeth over his lower lip. "The day before, 27th November, the *new* church, in the *new* Llanwddyn, was consecrated."

"But, likely, 28th November is the date I need."

"There is one more date..."

"Okay..."

"22nd November, 1889, was when the dam was considered to be filled."

"Well, that date had passed by the time the video was filmed, so I think that one irrelevant."

"I thought as much."

"Dr. Thomas." If Yvonne's gaze had been a laser, it would have cut right through the historian. "Is there any other event, that you are aware of, that might be significant at this time of year...specifically, now?"

"No." The shake of his head was emphatic.

"Thank you. Actually, I can't thank you enough."


Yvonne rose to her feet. Dewi, who'd been leaning quietly against the wall, was at her side.

"Dewi, let's get back to Newtown. Call the DCI and inform him of the need to rendezvous there, ASAP."

"Will do."

There was a real buzz about Newtown CID. They knew something big was on the cards, even if they didn't yet have all the details. The whole team was on edge but raring to go. Yvonne had been granted a special ops surveillance team for Lake Vernwy, due to the shear size of the lake and the task facing them. Her team would go on ahead, as soon as they were fully briefed. The operation was going to require every man Jack of them, and they were ready for it.

Yvonne pinned a large map of the lake area onto the board and waited for them all to settle down.

"I can't impress on you enough the urgency of this mission. If we get this wrong, Natasha Phillips won't make it." All eyes were on her. "We have every reason to believe that tomorrow is a significant date for the killer, and that is when he plans to drown the psychologist, if we let him. Some of you will be carrying out overnight surveillance in the area, and at first light, the rest of the team and special ops will be joining you."

"Most of you will be posing as walkers and tourists and we'll have aerial support, if he shows up." Yvonne rubbed the scar on her chin.

DCI Llewelyn moved to stand beside her, as though to reinforce having every faith in her intuition..

"He could be anywhere." Yvonne emphasised this fact by passing her hand over the map. "He may not have Tasha with him. Bear that in mind. I don't want anyone to move until we give the go-ahead. We've got to know his intentions before we do anything."

She paused, in order to look at all their faces. "Take food and hot drinks in your rucksacks. Stay vigilant. Don't put yourselves in danger. You'll be going in twos, in separate, unmarked vehicles - your own vehicles, if we don't have enough. Keep your earpieces turned on: special ops team will be advising you via them. They'll be calling most of the shots, at least until we locate the killer or Tasha. Make sure your hats and coats cover your equipment. Any questions?"

"What if he doesn't show? Isn't this all just based on a hunch?" One of the older DCs gave a sideways glance at Yvonne.

"If we're wrong on this, I'll take full responsibility for the failure. You're right in one sense, it is a hunch...but it's based on all the information we've gained about this killer, and on the few clues he gave us in the video. Let's face it, we have nothing else, and I, for one, do not wish to give up."

The DC nodded his acceptance.

"Go home, get some rest. I want all of you back in the station at 1.00 am, even those who will be staying behind, you'll be the ones liaising with uniform." DCI Llewelyn put a hand on Yvonne's back. "Thank you, DI Giles."

"God, I hope I've got this right," Yvonne sighed.

She and Dewi had stayed on at the station after the others left. They were about to greet Tasha's mother and father, and her partner Kelly. Yvonne had arranged it via the family liaison officer, who'd been keeping them informed ever since Tasha's disappearance. It was their wish to come to Wales. This meeting, and the possibility of ballistics getting back to them tonight, had meant the DI and Dewi would be getting any rest they could in the office.

Yvonne held Tasha's mum's hand. A green-eyed lady with greying-red hair in her early fifties. She had a quiet grace about her. When she spoke, the DI could hear the fear, barely held in check. Although Tasha's *voice* was her mother's, Yvonne mused that her friend's looks were definitely inherited from her dark-haired father. He, too, was greying, with a proud, square jaw and a cleft in his chin. He shook Yvonne and Dewi's hands, his face full of questions.

It was he who introduced the detectives to Tasha's partner.

"Detective Giles, this is Kelly..."

"Please," Yvonne smiled gently, "call me Yvonne...I'm pleased to meet all of you." She motioned to her detective sergeant. "This is Dewi Hughes."

"Pleased to meet you." He sounded tired, and a little hoarse. He coughed to clear his throat. "I'm sorry it's under such circumstances."

Kelly was just as Yvonne had imagined her from Tasha's description.    She looked every inch a strong business woman. Seemingly fiery and incisive, she had been on her mobile phone for almost the entire time she had been in the room.  It was clear, from the snippets of conversation the DI had overheard, that she was busy organising and doing deals, even now.  To Yvonne, it felt at odds with the situation. She mentally shrugged, it was none of her business.  Anyway, police stations were not like hospitals. Innocent civilians could use their phones, if they needed to.

All was peaceful, even serene, as Yvonne and Dewi approached Lake Vernwy, from the direction of the new village of Llanwddyn.  They passed a few walkers with their sticks and backpacks; a cyclist; a dog walker.  Nothing unusual.  And yet they knew an armed response unit was on its way from North Wales, a helicopter was on standby just over the border, and a surveillance crew, including members of their own team, were scattered around the lake, and could be any of the people they had seen on their way in.

They swung a left onto the bridge, over the dam walls.  The dirty-grey, lichen-stained Victorian architecture stood stark against the rolling hills, the forests and the watery expanse of the lake.

They were casually dressed, wearing jeans for one of the very few times in their careers. A distinct chill in the air meant the hats they wore to hide their earpieces didn't look out of place. No-one gave them a second glance as they left their car outside of the Vernwy cafe.

"I hope I'm right about this being the intended place, Dewi." She scanned the woods at the edge of the roadway, the bare trees scaffolding a mean-looking sky. Rain, though threatening, had so far failed to follow through. "If I've got this wrong..."

Dewi took in the worry lines, creasing her forehead. "This is the best chance she's got, ma'am, and it's down to *your* detective work." He rubbed his rumbling stomach. "They're advertising a hot chocolate in there, shall I get us a take out?"

"No, Dewi, let's go in: check who's around." She felt a relief of sorts, now that they had actually arrived at the lake. At least they could *do* something.

She shook her foot in an attempt to remove a clump of rotting leaves from her boot. "I hope he hasn't hurt her."

"I hope not, ma'am."

Yvonne took a seat at a round table, by the window. She could see who was coming and going outside and observe the few people already sat inside the cafe. She thought it unlikely the killer would come in here but, if he wanted publicity, he may be capable of anything. Whatever his intention, they were nearing his end-game.

She remembered what Dafydd Lewis' brother had said about Dafydd not wanting to work the family farm. Was that the sole reason he had entered the church?

The hot chocolate was thick with calories, smothered with marsh-mallows and whipped double-cream. She blew on the top, to enable her to take a sip. It was good. The sick feeling, in the pit of her stomach, had prevented her from having breakfast. The drink would, at least, help to raise her blood sugar enough for her to be useful. Dewi left, to avail himself of the men's room. She watched the pony-tailed girl who had served him wipe a spill from the counter-top and straighten the tins of exotic teas at the end nearest the window.

An older guy, with the air of being the boss, said something which the DI didn't quite catch, and the girl headed away from the counter and towards the back of the cafe. Yvonne's gaze moved on to a middle-aged couple eating toast and sipping on mugs of steaming beverage, a Collie sitting patiently on a lead beside them.

As Dewi returned, their earpieces kicked into life.

"The ARV is on-site, you now have armed back-up." It was Inspector Garside, from the Ops team. "Remember, the code word is RED."

Yvonne pursed her lips. 'RED' would be their confirmation he'd been spotted. Once that happened, she would have joint operational control, along with Inspector Garside of the Ops team. A trained negotiator was also on the way, and the DI was thankful for that. She tapped her mike. Dewi flinched. She turned her unit down a touch, grimacing at him. "Sorry..."

He looked almost as pale as the mug he set down on the table, and there were pronounced bags under his eyes, but her DS read her mind, rising with her as she left her seat.

"Are you okay, Dewi?" she asked, before opening the door.

"Right as rain, ma'am." He smiled, and stood to his full height. She heard his back click, but he didn't flinch. They walked out into the chilly, damp, November air.

To their left, stood a long, wooden cabin, comprising a bird hide. Ahead of them was the car park and, to the left, the road rose up, splitting right to go over the dam itself, and left to go around it. They were surrounded by trees. Yvonne turned towards the hide.

They entered the long cabin, fronted with glass windows, giving an almost uninterrupted view of the drop beneath. In front of the windows ran a row of seats and, to their left, a young German couple were holding hands and talking as they looked out. The DI put her forehead against the glass. A variety of birds were availing themselves of the feeders, and ground-lying tidbits on the small patch of horizontal ground out front. Yvonne peered down through the trees on the steeply falling bank, but saw nothing, save more mud, leaves and water. She felt a rush of impatience.

Dewi, taken by surprise, almost tripped as he saw her head for the door and turned to follow her. She stood in the car park, turning round and round, a frown furrowing her skin, her mouth open, billowing clouds of vapour. Finally, she walked towards the road, followed by her DS. They headed past the entrance to the dam bridge to their right, and the Lake Vernwy visitor's shop to the left, walking on for about a thousand yards to a small lay-by above the lake.

They walked to the edge of a little promontory to look out across the lake. A small cabin-boat sat on the water below and, on the bank to the left, stood a wooden hut - not that dissimilar to the one they'd just left. This one, however, had a red door and was obviously a boat house: a small row boat and a couple of lime-green canoes were tethered outside. The boat-house windows were small and impossible to see through from where they were standing, being around a thousand metres away.

Behind the boathouse were conifer trees and, beyond those, out in the lake rose a couple of towers, looking almost as though they'd been stolen from some French château, their conical roofs glinting with rain-reflected sunlight.

Vehicles were constantly coming and going, and many more walkers thronged around the cafe area. Yvonne sighed, the killer could be in any one of these cars. The easiest thing would have been to cordon off the whole area, but that would have alerted Tasha's kidnapper.

Walking back towards the road, she spotted a battered-looking pick-up truck parked partially on the verge. It peaked her curiosity and she walked over to Dewi and took hold of his hand, grinning at his raised eyebrows. "Just in case he's watching." She spoke low, through clenched teeth. Dewi smiled back, gave her hand a squeeze and swung her arm, as they headed towards the truck.

The pick-up was empty, save for a puddle of water in the back and a few odds and sods in the front: a flask, a sandwich box and pair of binoculars. Nothing of any note. They walked on, standing to the side whenever another vehicle passed. Yvonne could feel the cold beginning to penetrate every layer of her clothing, and found herself grateful for the warmth in Dewi's hand.

It was then she saw a figure below them, close to the boathouse. She felt the hairs on the back of her neck rising. "Who's that, Dewi?" she asked, fighting to relax her stomach muscles, willing the panic to stay away.

Dewi peered down, craning his neck to get a better view. "It's DC Clayton, ma'am."

She breathed again, DC Clayton was a member of her own team.


"CODE RED, CODE RED."

The call sent Yvonne's heart into orbit, he'd been spotted. Just as she was about to ask for confirmation and position, she saw a figure leaving the cabin in the boat below. She looked down to her right and saw DC Clayton standing stock-still, staring at the boat, his hands raised.

"Oh no, Dewi, he must have a gun..."

"No, ma'am." Dewi had already started to climb down the embankment to get a better look, and was breathless as he called back, "He's got a captive, and he's holding a knife to their throat!"

Yvonne caught up with Dewi, he having gone as far as he could towards the water, without falling in. She could see the hooded captive, which had to be Tasha, and, even though the killer was wearing a thick woollen hat, she knew immediately who he was. In control of the situation unfolding below, was Dafydd Lewis, the bishop of St. Asaph.

Yvonne grabbed the nearest branch and threw up down the bank, wiping her mouth with the back of her hand. "Everyone, stay back," she ordered via her microphone. "Where's DI Garside and the negotiator?"

She wasn't sure her last words had been heard, as there was a flurry over the radio. Garside was shouting instruction and calling for the ARV team to stand by.

Dafydd Lewis gesticulated from the boat, but she couldn't hear what he was saying. She saw DC Clayton wading out, towards the boat, stopping within metres of it. He threw something. Yvonne caught her breath.

Blue lights flashed at the far entrance to the dam and, from the wall itself, a loudhailer announced the presence of armed police, and ordered the hostage-taker to lay down his weapon. Like he was going to do that when *he* had the upper hand, Yvonne thought, but procedure was procedure.

They still didn't know what Clayton had tossed into the boat, but the bishop stood in the cabin-doorway, his knife still at his victim's throat. More flurry over the radio as Yvonne's ear piece started cutting out.

"Dammit!" She searched frantically in her bag for another earpiece. "Dewi, what's happening?"

Dewi concentrated on the flurry.

"Dewi?"

"One of the ARV squad reckons he has a clear shot, ma'am."

"Tell them no..."

"It's all right, Garside's telling them to hold their fire, to stand by and keep him in their sights."

"The man's got sense at least." Yvonne breathed again.


DC Clayton was making his way back up the bank, his feet slipping in the mud. Garside's car screeched to a halt in the layby, followed by two more vehicles. In the distance, Yvonne could hear a chopper on its way, and sirens echoing across the water.

"DI Giles?" DI Garside towered over her, but Yvonne was glad of his presence - not only because it made her feel less lonely in command, but Tasha was her friend, and she couldn't entirely trust herself to be objective.

"Yes, DI Garside?"

"It's Paul," he said, nodding towards the female heading towards them along the bank. She was far from suitably dressed for the conditions, her heels catching on rocks and tree roots. DI Garside continued. "This is..."

"I know who it is." Yvonne recognised the familiar features of Dr. Rainer, the occupational psychologist. "You're a trained negotiator? I didn't know..." She shot the words at Dr. Rainer, not meaning them to sound like an accusation.

She hoped the doctor hadn't spotted her white knuckles, or the shake in her offered hand. She turned her attention back to the man in the boat, and to the trussed and hooded form of her friend. She didn't know if Tasha was conscious or even alive.

DC Clayton joined them, still dripping, and shuddering from the cold. Dewi went to fetch blankets from the police vehicles on the bridge.

"He caught us off guard, ma'am." Clayton had a resigned look in his eyes. "Armed officers were only just arriving when he appeared in the boat. I was nearest to his position but I couldn't get there fast enough...the boathouse keeper had sworn the boat was empty and the cabin locked."

"How did he catch us off guard?" Yvonne struggled to hide her impatience. "There were officers dispatched just after midnight..."

"It's a huge perimeter," Clayton was frowning. "We were looking for the obscure places, sure that he'd pick a blind spot." He flicked his head in the direction of the boat. "But he chose the most bloody obvious place. I could kick myself."

The DI relented. "It's okay, you're not to blame. We all appreciate your efforts. You've been out all hours, in less than ideal conditions, with little or no sleep. What did you throw to him?"

"He's got my phone, ma'am."

Dewi arrived back with blankets, flasks of tea and hot soup. He almost dropped the flasks and Clayton ran over to save him. Dewi began pouring from one of the flasks. "Ma'am?" he asked, offering a mug to Yvonne.

She shook her head. "Not just yet, Dewi." She still couldn't face anything. Even though she was cold, she wouldn't *even* accept the offer of a blanket. It seemed traitorous for her to accept comfort, or sustenance, when her friend was down there, fearing for her life.

Yvonne checked that the position of the boat hadn't changed and rejoined Rainer and Garside, who were deep in conversation. After consulting with DC Clayton, Rainer punched some numbers into her mobile. The phone, on loud speaker, rang for several seconds before it was answered. Yvonne's hands were clenched, the knuckles white the entire time.

"Finally!" The Welsh lilt of the bishop was unmistakable on the other end. He was ready to do battle, Yvonne shifted between supporting legs.

"Do you need anything?" Dr. Rainer sounded calm, confident even, but the DI could see a light tremor in the hand holding the phone.

"What have *you* got?" The reply sounded, unsurprisingly, sarcastic.

"We've got blankets, sandwiches, soup?"

"None of the above."

Yvonne was straining to hear. "Can you ask him what he wants?"

Paul Garside nodded his support for the question.

Dr. Rainer paused, then: "If you change your mind, let me know." She was staring out at the occupants on the boat, as though wanting to see the bishop's expression. It wasn't readable from their position. "What is it you want, Bishop Lewis? Why are we all here?"

There was a moment or two of silence, then the sound of scuffling. Something was happening on the boat. It sounded like a struggle but, if it was, it was rapidly stifled.

The bishop's voice crackled out of the phone. "Are you Welsh?"

Dr. Rainer's voice was soft. "My grandfather was Welsh..."

"See?" His volume increased a notch. "I bet most of you up there are English. Everywhere I turn, this land, these people, all overtaken."

"You're angry with England?"

"I'm angry with the way our land and our people have been bled dry. A God-fearing people. An honest people. Lambs led to the slaughter."

"Why don't you let your hostage go? We can talk about your grievances."

"Talk? Since when did talking ever change anything? I've been talking all my life. Lately, less and less people have been listening. It's all gadgets and technology. It's not about individuals any more, and the rot started here, with these dams. With the whole industrial takeover driven by the English."

DCI Llewelyn was now in attendance, looking the most dishevelled she had seen him. Yvonne asked whether she might be allowed the phone. He shook his head emphatically. Through her earpiece, she heard a member of the ARV team assert, once again, he had a *clear* shot. It was her turn to vigorously shake her head. This time, the DCI and DI Garside nodded in agreement with *her*. DI Garside ordered his team to hold their fire.

She still felt shut out. Wasn't she the joint lead on this mission? It certainly didn't feel that way. Llewelyn and Garside were now so huddled together, she felt at any moment they would go down for a scrum. She waited for Llewelyn to break away and then dove in for the challenge.

"You're shutting me out..."

"Yvonne." The DCI sighed. "We're not shutting you out."

"You are, you *know* you are." Her eyes were two black pools.

"Look, I know how close you are to Tasha. It'll be hard for you to stay objective."

"Bullshit."

"It's not bullshit, Yvonne. Dr. Rainer knows what she's doing. If anyone can get the right result, she can. You have to trust her."

Yvonne had to admit she was still bitter about the enforced counselling with Rainer. She knew it was perverse, but she hadn't forgiven either the DCI or the psychiatrist. This seemed an invasion too far by the latter, and, yes, she was desperate to save Tasha.

"What would you like to see change?" Rainer continued.

"I'd like Wales to be independent. I'd like the church to be pure, the way it was. I'd like you lot to go back where you came from." The bishop yanked the head of his captive back, pulling off the hood.

"How is your hostage? Can we speak to her?"

Yvonne held her breath.

"She doesn't want to speak to you."

"Is she alive?"

At least Rainer was asking the questions Yvonne would have asked.

"She's alive, for now. Maybe ask me again in ten minutes." He gave a laugh which didn't sound convincing and Yvonne wondered, for the first time, whether the man in the boat was having a touch of self-doubt. In the distance, she could hear the swipe-swipe-swipe of the helicopter on stand-by, and knew it must be close. She was glad of its presence but frustrated by the level of noise. The thumping in her chest was a painful reminder of her desperation, and she fought the urge to throw up again.

Dr. Rainer continued. "Why don't you let the hostage go?"

226

A growl came from deep in the bishop's throat. He grabbed Tasha, and dragged her, roughly, to the edge of the boat. Now, fully visible, it was clear that not only was her head hooded and her hands bound behind her, but her ankles were also tied and a bag of something heavy attached. If he threw her over, she was dead. They'd never get to her in time.

"Wait!" Yvonne snatched the phone from the psychiatrist before anyone could stop her. "Dafydd, It's DI Yvonne Giles. I know they let you down, those people who dared to call themselves members of the clergy. They voted for female bishops and voted for gay people to wear the cloth. How could they have done that? Right?"

"Yvonne, what the hell are you doing?" Llewelyn's eyes flashed lightening at her. She didn't care.

The bishop paused at the edge of the boat, his victim held tight against him, his   knife to her throat. "They didn't deserve to wear their collars."

"Why did they even join the church?" she agreed.

"Probably didn't know what else to do with themselves. The words were delivered with a savageness, underlining his intent.

"You're playing a very dangerous game, Yvonne." The DCI threw the words from behind clenched teeth.

The DI handed the phone back to Rainer, and glared back at the DCI. "I'm sorry, sir, but he was about to throw Dr. Phillips in the lake, you know he was. We wouldn't get to her in time to save her. I think there's a problem with the bishop's mental health. I don't think he's rational. There's something more than just his beliefs going on here."

"You are not the trained negotiator." His tone was firm.

"The man whom Lewis' father and brothers describe is not the same man we are dealing with here. I think we should play to his tune for as long as it takes to get Tasha back safe. I also think we should find his estranged daughter." Yvonne looked over at Rainer and could see that she had support. This relaxed her a little, Rainer got it.

The officers from the North Wales and Cheshire Armed Response Unit were getting twitchy. More calls that they had a clear shot. The DI thought about the people she had met on that quiet, windswept farm in Pembroke. She really felt the bishop had a mental health issue. To kill him now would be to deny him treatment.

She grabbed DI Garside's arm. "Please, ask them to wait."

Once again, Paul Garside asked his team to hold their nerve. DCI Llewelyn took Yvonne to one side. "Look, don't think I don't know what you're going through. It's not really any different for us. We don't know what physical shape Dr. Phillips is in. At some point, someone is going to have to pull the trigger. It seems to me, Bishop Lewis came with one purpose in mind."

"I don't know...I don't know...can they really guarantee they won't hurt Tasha, if they take the shot? He's moving around quite a bit. He may be deranged, but he's not stupid. Anyway, I just thought we ought to give him a chance...a chance to get treatment."

"He killed Meirwen Ellis, he has come here with the sole purpose of killing Tasha, and doing it *very* publicly. Just look at the news teams, over on the bridge."

Yvonne looked over, and saw the throng, and sighed. Perhaps the DCI was right. Perhaps there would be no saving the bishop. Meirwen had been female and vulnerable, just like Tasha. Mental health or no, this man would have no compunction about dispatching another female.

Yvonne looked the DCI in the eyes. "Chris, we cannot risk Tasha's life."

"What do you suggest we do?"

"We've got a chopper on standby, right?"

"About a quarter of a mile away."

"What if we use it to get him off guard?"

"I doubt the noise would distract him for more than a millisecond, Yvonne."

"I meant fly it at him, or at least, fly it at speed across the lake, right over his head."

"What if he drops Tasha in the lake from shock?"

"Well what do *you* suggest?"

"I suggest we run your idea past Garside."


They were at it again, that little huddle, the DCI, Rainer and Garside. Yvonne sighed heavily.

When the DCI rejoined her, his gaze was intense. "We're going to go for it. We're going to bloody go for it. Are you sure you want to see this, Yvonne?"

"Yes. I'm not leaving."

DI Garside came over to Yvonne's side. He shook her hand and apologised for not having spoken properly with her earlier.

Dr. Rainer spoke into her phone. "Bishop, will you let us bring you and your captive back in? You'll have hot food, and can talk to us about your worries and grievances. We can get you help."

"I don't need help. I don't need anything from you. What I need is for governments to listen, for Wales to be properly independent, and for England to stop using Wales for its own ends. They'll be turning us into one big wind-farm next. I want to stop the selling off of church property, and all bishops should be males."

"Ask him why he killed his own clergy," DCI Llewelyn instructed Rainer.

"Bishop Lewis, will you tell us why you killed your own colleagues?"

"They were letting the changes in. Voting for them. Relaxing the rules over everything."

"What about Griff Roberts?" Llewelyn nudged Rainer. Yvonne knew this was to gain closure for the next of kin.

"Why did you kill Griff?" Rainer looked uncomfortable with this line of questioning.

"Griff Roberts? I thought he was my friend. He told me he was voting *against* the allowing of female bishops. He lied. He voted *for* them. I did the maths, the coward *must* have voted for."

Of course, Yvonne could see it now, Della Roberts had told her that Griff had been a lay-member of the church. So that was it, he'd voted for female bishops and sealed his fate.

**230**

DI Garside barked instructions to his team. From somewhere behind, Yvonne could hear the increasingly loud swipe–swipe–swipe of the helicopter. Dewi came and held her arm. She was grateful, he knew how to reassure her.

"Can we bring you in, Bishop?" Rainer asked again.

"It's time." The bishop stood fully up in the boat, hoisting his captive to the edge. His words were drowned out, as the chopper whirred overhead, shooting out over the lake, directly above the cabin-boat.

It worked: the bishop ducked, loosening the grip on his captive, who took her chance to pull away.

One shot. One shot rang out over the lake. The bishop dropped. No further movement was seen from him.

Yvonne felt relief and sadness, there were no winners in a situation like this, and yet she was glad for her friend. The shaking, which she had worked so hard to hide, was no longer controllable, and she sat on the ground, shivering.

A call came through on Dewi's mobile and he moved back, to a quieter spot, to take it. The news he relayed was no surprise to them now.

"It's ballistics, ma'am. The gun we found in Pembroke is the one that killed Griff Roberts and George Jones."

231

**TWENTY- FIVE**


Kelly was cutting deals again, her face animated as she negotiated, over her mobile phone, in the hospital restroom. Yvonne finished her coffee and waved at her, heading in the direction of the corridor that would take her to Tasha's bedside.

The grin which met her couldn't have been wider, and Yvonne matched it with one of her own. Running to her friend, she gave her probably the biggest hug she'd ever given anyone.

"You were pretty impressive out there." Tasha pushed at Yvonne's arm.

"I was?"

"Acting like you supported his stance on female bishops."

"You heard that?"

"Sure, the phone was on loud-speaker. I heard pretty much everything...well, bits of everything. It was clearer when he took my hood off."

"I got impatient."

"I had a feeling you would."

"I thought it the best chance of bringing him in alive."

Tasha gave a wry smile. "I know. I feel it too...the sadness. The whole sorry mess, such a waste of life, both for the victims and the perp."

"I'm probably on disciplinary." Yvonne pulled a face.

Tasha laughed inspite of herself.  "You never learn..."

"Says you, who took the hump with the DCI and went looking for trouble at Llyn Celyn."

"I didn't know if you'd been involved in that decision. I was more annoyed with you than the DCI."

"Not guilty. I gave the DCI what for, when I found out."

"I thought you would.  After I'd cooled right down, I knew you wouldn't have supported his decision. I was so bloody-minded, going off like that."

"You took a helluva risk."

"Says you, who got yourself kidnapped by the '*Sadist*'."

"Guess we're one-all..."

"Touché."

"Not funny."

"We've got to promise not to go risking ourselves like that again...ever."

"Think we'll get to work together again?"

"Of course..."

"Fine by me." Yvonne laughed.  "How long will you be in for?"

"Hoping to be out tomorrow.  They're treating me for dehydration and a cracked collar-bone. Other than that, I'm good to go."

They were making light of it, but when their eyes met, there was a shared understanding of what they had been through. They were sat in a comfortable silence, lost in their own thoughts, when Kelly walked in, apologising for having been away so long. Yvonne decided it was time to go, and squeezed her friend's hand before leaving the ward.

A week later, Yvonne was having morning coffee with Dewi.

"I still haven't properly caught up on my sleep."  Dewi finished his drink, leaning  back in his chair.

"I'm feeling better than I was." Yvonne replied. "But a mini-break might be in order."

They were about to exit the tea-room when a smiling Tasha, fresh from the hospital, came through the door and plonked herself down. "Too late for coffee?" she asked, fake pouting.

"Put the kettle on, Dewi, we'll have another one," Yvonne giggled.

"I've been looking at the pathologist's report, for Dafydd Lewis." The smile had disappeared from Tasha's face.

"The DCI let you *do* that?"  Yvonne was open-mouthed.

"A copy was given to Rainer, I sweet-talked *her* into seeing it..."

"Oh, you *did*, did you? *I* haven't even seen it, yet." Yvonne placed her hands on her hips.

"You probably won't now," Dewi interjected.  "The case is closed."

"Well, yes, I suppose it is." Yvonne turned her attention back to Tasha.   "What are your thoughts?"

"It's suspected that the bishop suffered with epilepsy."

"Epilepsy, really?"

"Yes, really. It comes in a myriad of forms and strengths, but the bishop may have had a mild case which can turn a normally easy-going person into an obsessive fanatic."

"And it had been undiagnosed?"

"It usually develops in later life. A sufferer can change from someone who is laid-back, with not a care in the world – no particular proclivities - to someone who will stand on street corners, trying to convince all-and-sundry to see the world from their new-found point-of-view. They go through an 'enlightenment', and want to convince everyone else they ought to go through it, too."

"Are you on the level, here?" Yvonne asked.

"Straight up. The really sad part is that with medication, the sufferer can lead a completely normal life: no obsessions, no shouting from the roof-tops, no murder-sprees."

"So, if our bishop's condition had been recognised, there would have been no victims...all those people...still alive."

"Absolutely."

"Were GPs negligent?"

"Not at all. In order to be diagnosed, you've got to present with symptoms, go see your GP, and be referred to a specialist etc. Thing is, Bishop Lewis lived alone. He saw his family, but only every now and again. There was no-one to spot what was going on, and suggest he see a doctor."

"I see..."

"Other people are our mirrors. We see ourselves through their eyes. Their reactions give us insight into who we are, how we come across."

"And for that to happen, there's got to be someone noticing the change."

"Exactly." Tasha gave a sad smile. "Various members of the clergy - vicars, vergers, Griff Roberts – knew something wasn't right, but didn't see enough of the bishop's general behaviour, or know enough of his past, to put the pieces together."

Yvonne leaned forward, elbows on the table, her hands wrapped around her mug, eyes watching the swirling patterns ebb and flow on the surface of her drink. Finally, she leaned back in her chair, looking from Tasha, to Dewi, and back again. "We've learned so much from this case, and now we learn that our killer was, perhaps, also a victim. I hadn't allowed for that, until those last few minutes, there on the lake. I'd gotten used to thinking of him as evil. I hope all of those who died rest in peace."

"Amen," Dewi and Tasha said in unison.

**THE END**

Printed in Poland
by Amazon Fulfillment
Poland Sp. z o.o., Wrocław